VAMPIRE
EMPRESS

/ / / /

J.R. RAIN
&
MATTHEW S. COX

THE VAMPIRE FOR HIRE SERIES

Moon Dance
Vampire Moon
American Vampire
Moon Child
Christmas Moon
Vampire Dawn
Vampire Games
Moon Island
Moon River
Vampire Sun
Moon Dragon
Moon Shadow
Vampire Fire
Midnight Moon
Moon Angel
Vampire Sire
Moon Master
Dead Moon
Lost Moon
Vampire Destiny
Infinite Moon
Vampire Empress

Published by
Crop Circle Books
212 Third Crater, Moon

Printed in the United States of America.

ISBN: 9798681426523

Chapter One
Unfair

Resigned to the whim of fate, I walk to the edge of the charred patch of ground and stare out at the jungle.

I'm almost upset at the animals out there for being unaware of what happened here. Perhaps a little jealousy on my part. They say ignorance is bliss, but animals are happy right up until something kills them. I wonder if pigs love the farmer the way dogs feel about their owners. Do they understand they're going to be betrayed at some point? What's the last thing to go through a pig's mind before it's slaughtered, other than a bullet?

Why am I even thinking this, being jealous of jungle birds and monkeys? It's not their fault I'm about to do something reckless and dangerous. There's too much on my mind for me to trust myself making any big decisions. Too much emotion and adrenaline—or whatever passes for adrenaline in my body now. Guess since I'm technically alive again and my body does seem to need actual food, maybe adrenaline is more than a metaphor.

So, yeah. Venezuela.

Freakin' Elizabeth.

She's seriously pissed me off in two big ways. Well, three, but her plan to take over an entire alternate world isn't as in my face as what she did to my kids. She threw us all—me, the kids, Allison, Kingsley, the creators she kidnapped, and some light warriors—into what people have been calling an 'eternity prison,' essentially a fake dimension floating out in the empty space between permanent dimensions.

Things are getting confusing here since everyone's calling different things 'dimensions.' There are two meanings to the word. First, the vertical meaning. The entirety of all creation exists as a series of 100 dimensional planes. Being a mere human—or at least having the brainpower of one—it's impossible for me to see their true arrangement, but suffice to say they're kind of like a column standing on top of each other like a pile of boxes. Earth, our reality, is on the third dimension. With each dimension one goes 'up,' things get exponentially more powerful... and weirder. For example, creatures native to the ninth dimension can mentally alter the realities of dimensions below them. Super advanced crap. Anyway, the 100th dimension is where the Origin resides. As far as I know, the 100th

dimension *is* the Origin.

So, that's the up and down concept.

In addition to talking about one-to-one-hundred, the word 'dimension' is also used to describe going sideways within the same vertical level. Think of it like a tall filing cabinet with 100 drawers. Earth, our world, is in the third drawer up from the floor. Inside our drawer, there exists an infinite number of folders. Each of those folders represents an alternate reality containing the entire universe we can see. All solar systems, planets, galaxies, and so forth straight out to the theoretical leading edge of matter expanding from the Big Bang. All of it fits into our third-dimensional folder.

Beings can survive on any dimension they are native to. For instance, a third dimensional being, like a human, can go sideways as far as they want as long as they stay inside the third drawer. Going up has bad effects, more severe the further from level three one goes. The worst effect is typically complete disintegration. It happens much faster the farther from home one goes vertically.

Going down has other problems. One doesn't risk disintegration, but de-volution. A higher dimensional being going down becomes weaker, starts to lose their powers, may lose intelligence, and could end up trapped with no way to go back where they belong.

However, as long as we stay in our respective drawers, we can go, say, two lateral dimensions over or *two million* away from where we were born without suffering crazy side effects.

So this eternity prison sat in the dead space between these 'folders' in the third drawer. By means of magic way beyond my understanding, while our physical bodies floated inside tiny prisons, our souls, spirits, ghosts, or consciousness—whatever you want to call it—were shot out across the third dimensional level into other alternate realities. Elizabeth found a way to throw us into worlds quite like ours, which happened to be aligned chronologically with painful or significant moments in the lives of our alternate selves. Time is a constant, but dimensions aren't necessarily all on the same page.

For example, in one dimension, it's still 1983 when I was only nine. The Sam there is nine, too.

See, with an infinite number of possible realities, it's almost guaranteed that some worlds will exist where a highly similar set of circumstances produced a highly similar situation. For example, a woman named Samantha Radiance Sundance married a man named Danny Moon—and weird crappola happened to them—in at least 1,432 separate realities. Elizabeth forced our astral selves to visit these other worlds while our bodies remained locked inside crystal prisons. I'm still not completely sure what her goal was. No, I do know. It was meant to distract us... possibly forever.

Prison indeed.

And each reality I visited felt an awful lot like some kind of test or video game scenario which I escaped only after taking some action that 'solved' the scenario. Once I got the answer correct, my astral self leapt to another world. Since it doesn't make any sense for Elizabeth to 'test' us, my guess is she either wanted to mess with our heads or keep us overwhelmed with grief, fear, panic, or helplessness. Again, forever.

Such a bitch.

Something else I considered. Sitting in an inter-dimensional prison is undoubtedly a strong risk factor for developing insanity, so she likely had to keep our minds busy. I figure as soon as someone goes insane, they probably can't be trapped in a dimensional prison... and somehow slip out.

Regarding me. No, I didn't break out *because* I went insane. I broke out to *avoid* going insane. And to stop Elizabeth. Her prison had been highly effective. Only myself, Anthony, and Max managed to escape on our own. Fortunately, we broke everyone else out on our way to the exit before the whole place collapsed.

Back to why I'm pissed at her.

The many, many reasons why I'm pissed at her.

Tammy's experience involved meeting a fourteen-year-old version of herself in a reality where both me as well as Anthony had died, and Danny turned into a sleazeball manager of an adult strip club who ran the women like prostitutes while claiming not to realize 'such things went on there.' The Tammy from said reality crashed hard, becoming a drug-using wild child totally out of control and… my Tammy happened to land there on the day the poor girl got herself killed during a high-speed police chase.

If the creator, Quentin, is to be believed—and my fingers are crossed he is—he's modified that reality so my death there had been faked by me, in an effort to conceal having become a vampire. With any luck, alternate Tammy won't be dying in a gruesome traffic accident... and will meet me again soon. I sure hope 'alternate me' can talk her down.

But I'm not pissed at Elizabeth for that, though. The events of an alternate reality would have played out the way they played out regardless. No, I'm pissed at her for making Tammy *witness* herself in such a state. She now believes the only reason *she* didn't end up in the same situation is me. And… the scary part is, if I'd listened to Danny soon after becoming a vampire and actually left, pretending to die… it's frighteningly likely the same thing would have happened here, too.

So, my daughter is mildly traumatized, full of guilt over her stint as a surly teen. The guilt and trauma have caused her to get clingy. I don't think she's going to regress and become totally dependent on me. Sure, she will be brittle for a bit, but I'm certain she will get past it. Still, for the moment, I'm furious at Elizabeth for damn near breaking her.

The second thing I'm mad at her for is what happened to Anthony. His situation is, admittedly, tamer than my daughter's. Plus, Anthony is—no secret here—mentally tougher. Tammy's a critter of emotion. Anthony's more logical. He's got plenty of emotions, too, but he's not ruled by them. They do sometimes overpower him when real bad stuff happens, like death. Or loss. His experience in the eternity prison sent him to an alternate reality where he got to witness another version of our family where his seven-year-old self was about to die of the same illness he nearly died from in my reality.

Danny, who'd been living inside my son as a sorta-dark master, decided he couldn't bear to watch alternate Anthony die as a little boy... and made the leap, turning the kid into a sorta-vampire. My son accepted the loss of his father for a second time because he thought it would be selfish to cling to Danny and not let him help the other version of our family.

So, there's that. Danny's finally gone. In a way, I'm relieved he's no longer inside my son's head. In another way, I'm pleased he's not even in our reality anymore. In yet another way, I'm a tiny bit sad—mostly for Anthony. Since the day I changed him into a vampire and back again to keep him from dying at seven, he's only cried three times: the first time Danny died, when Jacky died, and now... when Danny's spirit left him. Not to say my son's robotic. He has plenty of positive emotions. But it takes a *lot* to make him cry. And for doing it to him again, I'm angry with Elizabeth.

Honestly, hearing Tammy talk about watching 'alternate Danny' sit on her bed and break down thinking he'd lost her and wanted 'his little girl' back, almost made me feel sorry for him. Almost. The fourteen-year-old version of her had a good point. He could have easily walked away from being a sleaze king if he *really* cared about her as much as he claimed.

Speaking of the creators, I teleported them home already. It was kinda wild meeting Lance Black-burn, A-list Hollywood director, in person. In better circumstances, I'd have totally fangirled all over him. Also in better circumstances, Tammy would've been fangirling over Quentin Arnbury, the author of the *Contest of Sovereignty* novels, upon which the recent HBO drama series was based.

She's a bit too rattled to process things as trivial as adoring a fiction author. Well, perhaps more than simple fiction. See, Quentin's a creator, so the stuff he writes comes into being in an alternate dimension. Guess where Elizabeth's eternity prison sent him? Fortunately, we couldn't die in the alternate worlds. If we failed to outwit the 'scenario,' it merely reset. Poor Quentin suffered the wrath of his characters once they realized who he was. Tammy, after peeking into his head, said they kept executing him in various ways characters in the books had died—some of which were horrendous.

Quentin has since revised his opinion on character death, torture, inappropriate familial relationships, and such after experiencing that. However, I doubt he's going to go *too* far in the other direction. It's in him too deep to write his characters' deaths for drama, but he probably won't kill off twenty different beloved characters in each novel anymore.

The third thing hanging heavy on my mind is Elizabeth herself.

She originally kidnapped the creators in hopes of forcing them to make her an entire custom world out of thin air, suited to her whims in every way. She'd hoped to go there, bringing all her dark master allies, and live out her dream of being god-empress. At first, I'd been okay with this idea since the world wouldn't have existed without her... but I found out she'd have needed to keep the creators imprisoned forever to preserve the reality's existence. It didn't matter though, the plan failed.

So Elizabeth decided to jump to a 'real' alternate dimension, not one propped up by the imagination of creators. She apparently chose one like ours from about 2,000 years ago, before anyone invented modern weapons. Much easier to take over and dominate a primitive civilization than one capable of dropping atomic weapons on her vampire army.

We almost stopped her from invading the other world. Almost.

Stupid eternity prison.

Maybe it's partially my fault for killing the Red Rider and increasing the power level of magic in our world, but sorry... that monster needed to be destroyed. I get real funny about those who hurt children, and the majority of the Red Rider's victims hadn't turned eighteen yet. He'd been a witch hunter hundreds of years ago and, as they say, got a taste for the killing. The bastard also got a taste for siphoning off the magic from each of his victims. He even killed me in a prior mortal life, but I don't remember it—mercifully. His killing methods were far from pleasant or quick.

Elizabeth knew how I tend to go all mama bear about kids in trouble, so she—rightfully—figured I'd hunt down this Red Rider with great vengeance and furious anger, or whatever the saying is. And I did.

Anyway, point is, magic is back on Earth, and it gave Elizabeth the power to fling us into the eternity prison at a critical moment when we attacked her. Max, a group of Light Warriors, myself, my kids, Allison, and Kingsley all did our best to stop her from invading the other reality—but we failed. Elizabeth slipped through and is already doing who-knows-what there.

Max and about half his Light Warriors escaped the eternity prison due to protective spells they wear to guard against unwanted teleportation. When Elizabeth dropped the wormhole bomb on us—my word for it since I don't understand it at all—Max and about sixteen of his people boomeranged across the aether and landed back in California at his library. The other dozen or so Light Warriors who survived fighting the ascendant dark masters made a separate escape from the eternity prison, but didn't realize red portals went to other alternate dimensions belonging to other prisoners. So, it took Max a little longer to find and pull his people out of the alternate worlds they landed in.

So, now... Max and the warlocks, witches, or whatever they call themselves, working with him, are trying to open an interdimensional gateway to the same place Elizabeth went by tracing the lingering magical strands or some such thing. When I said I'm resigned to the whims of fate, I meant this: if their portal works, I'm going to rush through it and try to stop Elizabeth. Doing so could result in me being stranded or permanently stuck in some other reality—assuming Elizabeth doesn't destroy me entirely. If Max and his people fail to open the gateway and determine it's impossible to find her... then we cede defeat and spend a while mourning all the people who will suffer under her rule.

Alas, it will have been a 'we did everything we could' situation.

Except I know me... I will continue looking for ways to stop her. After all, I got a hella long time to figure it out.

For the time being, I sigh, pull out my phone, and glance at the time. In a normal life, I'd be sitting at home watching *Judge Judy* now. Even in my not-so-normal life, I'd be watching *Judge Judy* now if not for the need to chase the bitch across dimensions.

Normal. What does that even mean anymore?

I saw different versions of what my life might have been, like the one where I'm thirty-seven and Anthony's dead because I never became a vampire and couldn't save him. Danny's also dead because he couldn't handle the grief of losing our son… and I ended up raising my sister's three kids because Elizabeth made *her* the vampire and she disappeared to protect us.

No, I don't wish my life had been different from what happened. But it doesn't mean I can't enviously daydream about an ideal reality where no vampire stuff happened, Anthony didn't get sick at age seven, and the Moon family got to enjoy plain old boring, happy normal. My life has swerved so wildly off the tracks, I can't even begin to guess what my kids would've been like in such an ideal world. Anthony probably would've ended up in a career with computers or a mundane office job. Tammy… might've become a veterinarian or a vet tech. Maybe even a teacher or an artist. I could see her turning into that eccentric art or history teacher all the kids like but the parents keep questioning if she's qualified.

Gee, thanks, Mom.

I chuckle.

Tammy walks over and leans against me.

I ask, "What do you think you'd have done if we had an ordinary life where nothing went wrong?"

"Hmm." She kicks her sneaker at the dirt. "I can't even think of anything. Probably wouldn't have been into goth stuff. I think it happened because my mom was a vampire. I wanted you to see me being into gloomy, dead stuff so you knew I wasn't afraid of you and thought you were cool, not as lame as you thought."

"Wait. I thought I was lame?"

Tammy laughs. "You're lame because you're a parent of a teenager, but you're cool. And it's false lameness. All teens call their parents lame. I don't mean it as in you are actually lame."

"Right. I get it. I think. How are you doing?"

"Still freaking out. But holding it in. Is it more abnormal for you to have wings or me to only be a week into being eighteen and thinking like I owe everything to my mother?"

"Hard call. Usually, daughters and moms don't become best friends until the kid's in her early thirties. But there is always an outlier."

"Like you." She rests her head on my shoulder. "You don't even talk to your mother anymore."

"I didn't really talk to her much as a child, either. Like I said, outlier."

"Aunt Mary Lou is more like your mom."

"I suppose. But she feels like my big sister."

"A good thing?"

"Yes, a wonderful thing."

She nods, pauses. "Mom?"

"Yeah?"

Tammy looks me in the eye. "Ant thinks we're gonna be okay."

I smile. "He's a good kid."

"No, I mean he really thinks we're going to be okay. He hasn't seen what Elizabeth can do."

I narrow my eyes. "Elizabeth hasn't seen what *I* can do."

Anthony walks up on my left side. "You guys doing okay?"

"Yeah," we say simultaneously, then, "Not really."

"Something wrong?" asks Anthony. I sense the kid's need to protect us, to make things right.

"Nerves mostly." I exhale.

"By the way," says Tammy, "Elizabeth lied."

Anthony fake gasps. "Shocker."

I point at him, look at Tammy. "What he said. Specifics?"

"What she told you before, about Max. She didn't have the chance to kill him and hesitate because he's her son. It went the other way. *He* had her on the steps of some big temple somewhere far back in time, a knife at her throat… but *he* couldn't do it. She pretended to love him but almost killed him when he lowered his guard."

I shudder. "Damn. There I go having too much faith in a mother's love."

"Umm, Mom?" asks Tammy, pulling her hair out of her eyes. "Speaking of crappy parents…"

"Uh oh." I fake cringe. "You wanna go see my folks?"

Tammy bites her lip. "Not where I was gonna go with this, but if you think it's a good idea, I'll do it."

"We can cross that bridge later. What's on your mind now?"

"Ant and I were talking already, and… we're totally cool with it if you wanna foster that Paxton kid."

"Say what?" I blink.

"Sorry, you've been thinking about her a lot in the back of your mind." Tammy exhales. "She's scared and lonely."

"Um, wow. Yeah, I'm worried. That poor girl's not in a good environment."

Tammy nods. "Yeah. When she said that thing about if she had a mom like you, she was actually hoping you'd want to adopt her because you didn't freak out about her being, you know, into girls."

That poor kid. I'm *so* tempted to find her father and see how he likes being thrown down stairs. True, I've been worrying about her whenever I haven't been flipping out over the Elizabeth craziness… which means there hasn't been too much time spent worrying about her.

"I don't know if it's fair to her," I say. "Our lives are crazy."

"Yeah." Anthony smiles. "But still fun."

Tammy rests a hand on my shoulder, staring into my eyes. "Mom, what's unfair is leaving a vulnerable kid like her at the mercy of the system. If she gets a bad foster family, they're going to mess her up for life. Being in a family who occasionally deals with demons, vampires, werewolves, and such is not a big deal at all compared to awful foster parents."

"And, we're just saying it's okay with us if you want to." Anthony stretches, trying to act casual, like he doesn't want to run straight back to Fullerton and play bodyguard for her.

Tammy obviously knows how close I came to scooping Paxton up like a kitten at an animal shelter and walking out the door with her. As much as that girl yanked on my mom instincts, it's not going to matter at all if we don't survive this.

"Mom..." Tammy cling-hugs me. "Don't think like that. Stay positive."

Anthony puts an arm around my back. "I won't let her hurt you, Ma."

I hate to say it—well, not really—but with Danny gone, Anthony seems visibly happier. His smile is wider, eyes brighter. No matter how much my *very*-ex-husband may have loved his son, he was still a dark master, a significant source of negative energy.

Tammy nods at me. *I see it, too. I'm sad for him his link to Dad's gone, but he's better off.*

Footsteps approach from behind us at a casual gait, no attempt to be stealthy. Since I don't feel threatened, I don't whirl around.

"Are you three ready?" asks Max. "I believe we are prepared to open the gateway."

We all turn to face him more or less at the same time.

"We're ready," I say.

Chapter Two
A Little Different

It would be a lie for me to say I didn't have a tiny bit of hope Max would fail.

Seriously. Who *wants* to jump into another dimension? I'm not superhuman—well, okay, *physically* I am—but my psyche isn't. Samantha Moon is every bit as susceptible to fear, self-doubt, pessimism, and dread something will happen to her children as any other mom. It's not that I'm afraid of confronting Elizabeth, even though I really ought to be. If Max and his people can't open this portal, we're going to be stuck unable to get involved. Then, I won't have to worry about my kids being hurt or ending up stranded in some other world where no one understands the concept of light bulbs.

Anthony wouldn't be able to go three days without his online game. I'd make a joke about

Tammy and a world without cell phones, but she's kinda tame in that regard compared to the stereotypical teenage girl. Not like she needs a phone to talk to her friends miles away. She never turned into one of those girls who spends hours on phones. Honestly, she could use telepathy but prefers to keep her psychic abilities secret from them.

Tammy's understandably scared. Considering she is the most normal person here, it also makes her the bravest for being willing to go. The Light Warriors have magic to defend themselves. Max has his alchemical creations, magic of his own, and centuries of experience. Allison has magic. Kingsley's a freakin' werewolf. I'm... something. Anthony's got the Fire Warrior.

My daughter can read minds. Not exactly going to protect her if a vampire gets in her face.

However, her role here is both critical as well as one she can fulfill miles away. She'll be hiding everyone from Elizabeth. Alchemists love using elemental magic... and surprise is an element.

Okay, maybe it isn't scientifically an element, but you know what I mean.

A group of Light Warriors assemble in a circle around lines and symbols they've etched in the ground. Max stands off to the side, talking to Allison like a professional musician giving another professional musician a rundown of the chord progression before they attempt playing a song they've never tried before. Her nodding along with him gives me confidence and worry in equal parts.

Got a feeling this is going to work. Another feeling tells me we're about to take a trip that will make our European vacation feel like an actual vacation. This won't be as easy as stomping out a few fire imps.

Anthony is pretty confident. Unlike me, who *looks* confident but has a bit of worry inside. Tammy is neither confident nor looks it. Kingsley seems bored. He's got his hands on his hips, looking around at everyone with a 'can we get this over with? I have a meeting at two' expression.

A young Light Warrior—and by young I mean the guy's about twenty-two—rushes over to give Tammy a modern compound crossbow and a nylon bolt case. She takes them out of reflex, staring at the retreating man like 'what the hell am I supposed to do with these?'

I put an arm around her. Those are silver bolts, hon. If you—

If an ascendant dark master finds me, I'll never see them fast enough to use this thing. Besides, I have no idea how to fire a crossbow.

"Easy," says Anthony. "Crossbows are the first point-and-click interface."

"Video game reference?" I ask.

My son sighs. "Yes, ma."

Meanwhile, Allison nods at Max, then runs halfway around the circle to take her position. I stand with the other non-magic people near the edge of the ring of Light Warrior mystics. Of the twenty-seven men and women left in Max's 'army,' nine of them are skilled in magic. The rest are kinda like monks. They have magic, too, but channel it inward. When fighting demons, vampires, or other monsters, their spells make them stronger, faster, tougher… able to take on superhuman fiends and not be swatted aside like fleas.

A few cluster by Anthony, surprising me by saying things like 'glad to have you with us' or commenting his presence makes them feel more confident. Okay, when did my fifteen-year-old (soon to be sixteen-year-old) become Master Chief?

Whoa, Mom, says Tammy in my head. *Did you just make a Halo reference?*

I think I did. I smile at her.

Since when do you play video games?

I don't. But I've seen your brother play Halo often enough to make a joke about it.

By the way… many of them see Anthony has something… greater.

Greater how?

I'll tell you later.

Why not now?

Because it's starting…

What's start—

My thoughts are cut off as the wizards, alchemists, or whatever they are, begin chanting. Allison does as well, reading from a little card Max must've given her. Speaking of Max, he walks around the interior of the circle, sprinkling powdered gold and silver into the lines of the ritual circle.

A few minutes go by of chanting and drawing magical symbols on the ground in powder.

Anthony walks up to the edge of the circle for no particular reason, standing there like he's posing for a *Superman* movie poster.

What the heck is he doing?

Mom, he's not sure either. Just felt like he needed to help.

Help? Your brother's no magic-user.

Tammy gives me a blank look. *Ant doesn't know either. He's got this weird idea, like he can help open the portal if he wants it to open. He's kinda just standing there wanting the portal to work.*

Okay, power of hope, I suppose?

Maybe.

Max backs out of the circle to join the ring of Light Warriors. He pulls a gold coin from his pocket and flips it into the air, away from him. The coin flies into the circle, stopping in midair at the center, where it continues spinning, faster and faster until it looks like a tiny ball. Yellow lightning crackles from the spinning coin. The golden orb rapidly expands to the width of a bus, then hollows out to a thin ring surrounding a pale sandy-brown haze. The blur sharpens to a flickering image of the desert, like one of those ancient hand-crank movie machines with the paper cards.

Gradually, the shifting effect stops. It's like watching a 1920s television image morph into modern high-definition, one of those screens so real you'd swear you could walk right into the scene. Only, here, we *can* walk into the scene. Warm air blows out of the opening, tossing hair and fabric about.

Well, heck. It worked. Here we go.

Anthony's the first to move, striding across the ritual circle and into the opening. Despite her worry, Tammy drags me forward, not wanting to be separated from her brother. I walk through, holding her hand, Kingsley right behind us.

Even though I'm still wearing the snowflake-sun amulet. Max gave it to me for protection against Alaska's cold, but it will also keep me cooler in a scorching desert. I get a brief blast of hot due to the sudden transition of environments before the enchanted item compensates and it feels like I'm once again at comfortable room temperature.

Ahead of me, rippling beige sand stretches all the way to the horizon, becoming a dune sea toward the left but staying relatively flat on the right. A large shape darkens the horizon in the blurry distance at a two-o'clock position. It's gotta be miles away, and huge. The generally pyramid-like form makes me think human-made rather than mountain.

I twist to look behind me, surveying the land. Allison, Max, and the rest of the Light Warriors step through the portal. More dune sea surrounds us to the rear, hazed by the shadow of a mountain range much farther away than the 'pyramid.' No signs of life, civilization, or Elizabeth are anywhere in sight.

"Wow, it's hot here," says Tammy. "Ant, I swear, if you say 'yeah, but it's a dry heat' I'm going to slap you."

He smiles cheesily. "Well, it *is* dry here. Venezuela was humid."

"Oh, interesting." Allison nudges me with her elbow, then shows me her iPhone. "Still kinda works, but I'm not getting a signal. It's 107 degrees."

Tammy groans at the temperature.

"Your fault for wearing black shirts all the time," says Anthony to Tammy.

"Bite me."

Not sure if watching them act like kids is comforting or surreal considering where we are and why we're here. I point to Allie's phone. "So, why are you shocked it works?"

She shrugs. "Well, I kinda wondered if this being a primitive world with more magic than Earth might cause technology to stop working."

Max, standing next to Allison, chuckles. "The laws of reality do not change quite so drastically within the third dimension. Simply because they have not developed technology here does not mean technological items *cannot* work... but I do not think you'll find a place to plug it in."

Allison smiles. "Figured that."

"No tracks," says Kingsley, pointing at the ground. He raises his head, sniffing. "I don't smell them either."

"She's far away," reports my daughter. "I'll shield us again the closer we get."

"What is this place?" asks a male Light Warrior.

Max waves for everyone to gather around him. "As some of you already know, Elizabeth has chosen this dimension to invade. From what I have been able to determine thus far, it is highly similar to our world as it existed somewhere between two and three-thousand years ago. It is difficult to draw an exact comparison due to certain differences in our worlds. For example, magic is far more prevalent here. It most certainly has affected the development of their civilization in ways we did not experience."

Murmurs and nods come from the group.

Max holds up a hand-drawn map depicting continents, but they don't have any similarity in shape to the Earth I know. "We are presently in a region corresponding to what would be Egypt in our world."

"Explains the pyramid," says Tammy.

"But we're not *in* Egypt." Max smiles at her. "Our position on the globe is roughly equivalent. This is the region of the world with the most people and the most advanced civilization. It is no surprise she chose this place as it presents the quickest route to establishing an empire comparable to Ancient Rome."

"Rome fell, though," says a woman in a brown robe.

"Indeed." Max nods at her. "However, Rome was not under the control of a psychotic dark master with a small army of immortal warriors."

A Japanese woman, also wearing a brown robe,

lowers an honest-to-God spyglass from her eye and points. "There's a huge city in that direction, with a pyramid at the center."

Kingsley tugs at his collar, sweating like hell. As soon as I notice him overheating, Allison gets the hint over our mind link. She stops playing with her phone long enough to cast the same spell on him, herself, and the kids, she used to keep everyone from freezing in Alaska. She just reversed the effect... cooling rather than warming. If I'd known she could do that, I wouldn't have pestered Max for this amulet... but then again, a bit of jewelry is a lot easier to carry in my pocket than Allison Lopez.

Magic like that just seems so damn beyond me.

Anyway, Kingsley immediately looks relieved, and finger-shoots Allison a thank you. She grins and shoots him back. Anthony doesn't look much different, truth be known. My son has a sort of weird, zen-like expression on his face... like not much will bother him, especially not heat.

Meanwhile, Max approaches the Japanese woman. She hands him the spyglass, waiting beside him while he surveys the distant city for a minute or two before returning it. "This is the spot Elizabeth's portal touched. She will most certainly have gone to the city. It is indeed massive."

"How didn't they all burn to death?" asks Tammy. "And there's no tracks."

"Footprints do not last long in the desert, child," says Max. "Wind erases them in hours. I suspect it had been dark here when they arrived. Probably a calculated move on her part. Easier to move around in the coolness of night."

Tammy glances at me. *He called me 'child,' but I'm eighteen now. Should I have a tantrum or ignore it?*

Feeling the intended joke on the thought wave she sent, I chuckle. He could call my grandfather's grandfather 'child' and still be correct.

Oh. Duh. Right. I forgot how old he really is.

Seriously.

Tammy bites her lip. *He's kinda hot.*

I stare at her. You did not…

Come on, Mom. Look at him. Right up there with Zac Efron. I love his blue—huh? Are his eyes are green? I swear they were blue a second ago.

They change color.

Whoa. Oh, crap. They're violet now.

And stop crushing on Archibald Maximus.

Dammit, Mom! You ruined it.

What?

She faces me, arms out to either side. *Archibald? Seriously? That is like the most unsexy name ever.*

Great. First an elf, now Max. My daughter has a thing for older men. *Way* older.

She blushes. *Mom! Kai is my age, just in elf years.*

Yeah, that's going to get real awkward in a couple decades.

"We should get moving. Bad enough we're out here in the sun already." Max gestures at the distant city.

The portal behind us picks that moment to close.

We all stand there watching it shrink from a giant ten-foot disc down to a pinpoint. It took a little self-control not to dive through at the last second. Not much. Just a teeny amount. More like an instinctual reaction to jump off a sinking ship rather than go down with it. Again, who wants to be stranded in another reality? I wouldn't be human if self-preservation didn't at least emit an easily ignored squeak of protest in the back of my mind.

Honestly, I got the same twinge the few times I had to interview an inmate at a prison back in HUD. A door closing behind me that I can't open freaks me out. Hate feeling trapped. Anyway, Max and his people opened the gateway once, they can do it again—provided we're alive to leave.

Tammy gurgles. *Stop thinking bad thoughts!*

Max takes the lead, as casually as if desert hiking used to be a hobby of his. It's hard to wrap my brain around how long he's been alive. Back when Elizabeth had been a mortal human, maybe they *did* live in the desert. Sebastian's dark master is from Egypt. The mermaid Kingsley told me about... her dark master is from the same area, too. From like the year 30 A.D. or something ridiculous like that. Guess the Ancient Egyptians had a lot of people into blood magic who became dark masters.

We walk for a little over an hour before we spot the wreckage of a large creature-drawn wagon of some type in the sand ahead. Any variation in the scenery is super obvious since we're surrounded by the same pale sand. Increasingly taller dunes are to our left; mostly flat, rippled sand to the right. No sign of a coast or end to the desert in sight.

Several bodies lay partially buried around the smashed wagon, but no tracks or footprints give any indication of what happened here. The wagon's about the size of a school bus, but uncovered. Considering it's empty, my guess is it belonged to a trader of some kind and bandits raided it to steal the merchandise.

Max and the Light Warriors head over to the bodies.

Tammy averts her eyes, not wanting to see dead people, but relaxes once it becomes obvious the corpses are nothing but bones. Their clothing, mostly white or pale brown loose-fitting tunics, thawbs, or robes, is astonishingly free of bloodstains. Stylistically, they're a cross between ancient Arabia and Camelot.

Anthony jogs over to us holding something that looks like a lightsaber handle. "Hey, check this out."

Kingsley raises both eyebrows.

My son looks at the end while picking at a green gem on the side, suspiciously similar to a button.

"Don't look directly at it!" yells Tammy. "If that's a laser sword, you're going to... put your eye out."

Anthony aims the device away from himself and pushes the gem. Nothing appears to happen until he tilts it upward. The front end now glows, but the light's too weak to really notice in the desert daytime.

"Flashlight?" suggests Tammy.

"Yeah. Looks like it. But, there's no light bulb." He pushes the gem again, effectively turning it off, and tosses it to Tammy.

I slide over and take a look. The front end of the device is a smooth, mirror-finished bowl. As far as I can tell, nothing in it is capable of producing light.

"Whoa." Tammy pushes the gem, once again causing a tiny cloud of glowing energy to appear.

"Yeah, that's a flashlight all right." Kingsley scratches his head. "At least in function. A touch different than our world."

Anthony wags his eyebrows. "Don't you mean a *torch* different?"

Kingsley pinches the bridge of his nose and groans.

"Huh?" Tammy scrunches her face at him. "It's a flashlight, not a torch."

"We were just in London. They call 'em torches there," says Anthony.

I groan. Tammy merely sighs.

Max approaches us, carrying a bundle of fabric. "Here. You may wish to change into these so you don't stand out so much."

"Eww!" Tammy backs up. "Dead people wore those."

"It will not do us any good to advertise we have come from another place." Max sets the bundle on the ground in front of us. "If Elizabeth has spies around the city, they will know we're here as soon as they see your modern clothes."

I'm about to remark about him and all the Light Warriors, but their outfits are not as obvious as ours. Some are already wearing robes, the rest dressed somewhere between Indiana Jones and Allan Quartermain. They still look out of place here but not as obvious as logo T-shirts, jeans, and sneakers.

Allison and I sort the pile, laying each piece out on the sand. She uses magic to mend various slashes as well as holes likely from arrows (or crossbow bolts).

"This is beyond weird. There's bad energy in these," says Allison. "I think I know why none of this stuff has blood on it."

"Do tell?" Kingsley sniffs a thawb. "Doesn't smell like blood, but I'm getting a note of decay. Darn. Now I'm hungry."

Tammy grimaces, looking nauseated.

"I think these people were killed by magic that caused their bodies to decay instantly," says Allison.

"You want me to wear clothes that people died in and like rotted in seconds?" Tammy shivers. "Umm, no."

"We have to, Tam." Anthony play-punches her shoulder. "If they suspect we're from Earth, we could get caught."

"Eww. Eww. Eww." Tammy hugs herself. "I'd

rather strip and wear illusions than something rotting corpses touched."

"Relax." Allison smiles up at her. "I'm magically cleaning them now."

"You can do that?"

"No. But I thought it would make you feel better."

Tammy pouts. "I hate you."

Since we've got magic keeping us comfortable from the heat, we pull the native clothes on over our modern attire for now. Anthony puts on a tunic that stops halfway to his knees, then discreetly pulls his jeans off. I pull a robe on, as do Allison and Tammy —reluctantly. Kingsley, unconcerned with who sees what, strips down to his boxers and pulls on a thawb. His suit, all of our shoes, and Ant's jeans go into a large brown sack for now. Wearing the leather sandals of a dead guy is a bit bizarre, but Nikes would be a dead giveaway we're not from around here.

A few of Max's people with less time-period-ambiguous clothing grab the remaining cloaks.

Tammy looks over at me. *Is this place going to be dangerous for us, since we're women?*

I'm not sure. Relax. I'm not going to let anyone mistreat you. Or me. Or Allison.

She exhales shakily, but nods.

Anthony walks around in a circle, acclimating himself to wearing a tunic and sandals. "Feels like we're in a movie or something. Hope there aren't any mummies out here."

"Could be," says Max from a distance off, still examining smashed boxes. "Until we understand the extent to which magic is prevalent in this dimension, anything is possible within reason."

The Alchemists urge us to resume walking since there's nothing else worth salvaging. Whoever attacked the wagon stole everything, even the animals used to pull it. Everything is gone, except the one flashlight and the corpses.

"Ma?" Anthony walks up beside me. "Is this what it felt like when you got stuck in Talos's world?"

"No... not exactly." I smile. "Well, both places had tons of sand, but this is actually *much* nicer."

"Really?" He blinks. "How can anything be better than a world full of dragons?"

I laugh at his innocence. "Well, for starters, I don't have a constant fear of disintegration."

"Always a plus," calls Max from the front of the line.

"And we don't have to worry about dragons trying to eat us." Tammy gives me a 'yikes' look. She saw my memory of those razekh creatures... the dumber dragons only about as smart as dogs.

Max holds a finger up. "Be wary of speaking too soon. We do not yet know if this world has dragons or not."

Kingsley tosses and catches the magical flashlight. "And they make these things with magic. Who knows what we're going to find here."

"Eep," whispers Tammy.

Anthony puts an arm around my and Tammy's shoulders, walking between us. "We're doing the right thing, Ma. I got a feeling we need to be here."

"Glad someone's feeling confident," mutters Tammy.

"I'm confident, too," I say. "It's possible to be confident while appreciating the risks."

Anthony squeezes us a little tighter before letting his arms drop. "Not sure how to describe it, but I got this feeling something's big's gonna happen. Not necessarily bad. Just big."

I sigh. Truth is, I have the same feeling.

What that something is remains to be seen.

Chapter Three
Blending In

When we come within about three miles of the city, Tammy takes off her amulet and concentrates. She's not going all trancelike and weird though.

"I don't feel her yet," she says. "But don't worry, I've got the psychic equivalent of an umbrella up right now. As soon as I have to, I'll put more into it and someone will need to carry me."

"No prob," says Anthony.

After another hour of walking, the city's close enough to make out a huge defensive wall, with a crap-ton of tents circling the base of it. Most of the tents are as big as cabins, some rounded like teepees, others closer to small circus tents... the sort of things people put up at outdoor festivals to cover rows of cafeteria tables. It doesn't look like a transient caravan stopping in the shade of the city, but rather a separate district unto itself, a permanent outer-city arranged in a ring, a modest distance from the defensive wall.

I can't tell from this far away what the wall's made from other than stone of some kind. It's white and fairly smooth, having no cracks or seams between individual bricks. Kinda resembles adobe. Like a pyramid, the wall is angled inward, and looks about twenty-five feet tall based on the size of the soldiers patrolling on top of it.

While I've never claimed to be any sort of professional tactician, it doesn't make much sense to me for walls to be sloped like that. An athletic person could legit run straight up the side to the top if they got enough of a head start. Only reason I can think of is someone thought it 'looked cool.' Admittedly, the generally triangular shape of the city from a distance is kinda imposing, even if their fortification is more decorative than functional.

Guess they're not worried about land invasions being so far out in the desert. Moving an army to this place would be a colossal undertaking since I'm almost certain this world does not have aircraft or giant tanker trucks carrying water. Additionally, the lower parts of the wall have to be ridiculously thick, narrowing the higher up it goes. Battering it down would be a pain in the ass.

At the center of the bizarre wall stands a gate made of two dark brown slab doors. From here, they somewhat resemble wood, but only in color. They're presently open. A small cadre of soldiers stand guard in the relatively narrow passageway leading into the city. Seems like they are allowing people to freely come and go.

Tammy's still walking on her own, but she has a suspicious 'where are you hiding' expression. I'm guessing she kinda feels Elizabeth's presence, but can't exactly tell where she is. Telepathy is similar to sonar. Tammy and Elizabeth are two submarines playing chicken at the height of the cold war, listening for passive sounds. If either one of them sends out a 'ping,' the other will know the enemy is close.

Max leads us to the outskirts of the tent city, close but not going in too far. He wanders for a little while before stopping near an open space between two big, rectangular tents. Three of the robed Light Warriors who helped open the portal, two guys and a woman, stand in a row and raise their arms. They seem hesitant until Max nods, then they focus, chanting in Latin, I think. Swirls of sand kick up in the empty spot seconds before a large plain brown tent pops into being out of thin air.

"It worked!" The woman in the middle jumps back as if shocked.

The guy on the right stares in awe at his hand. Most of the remaining Light Warriors react with varying degrees of surprise. Max and Allison both appear largely unimpressed. Allison's a little surprised at the sheer size of the tent, but she's conjured physical objects into existence before… so this isn't *too* strange to her. Granted, the biggest item she managed to conjure pre-Red-Rider-blowing-up was a fountain pen. Magic in our world has gotten more powerful, but she's thinking this dimension is significantly more magic-rich.

Max ushers his people into the tent as if afraid of them being seen, then asks us to hide out in the tent as well. No real point to argue, so we go inside. Once done, he and one of the larger guys head out for a 'scouting trip.' Minutes later, a small group of robed Light Warriors decide to look for some water and head out. Good idea.

Allison, Tammy, and I sit on some conjured pillows, discussing how weird it is to be in an alternate reality chasing Elizabeth as well as trying not to freak each other out by wondering how dangerous she's going to be when cornered.

Anthony fidgets in a way that tells me he really wants to be playing a video game, or at least doing something. He looks bored, but also far too calm, like we're on another leg of our vacation about to watch a bunch of period re-enactors joust. Out of the blue, he walks over to the group of Light Warriors and joins their conversation, mostly about Max planning to open another gate to bring in additional reinforcements from the East Coast and Europe. They all seem to have the belief we're looking at a serious battle here, more or less a straight up war.

Ugh. I really hope not. And it's strange hearing multiple people talk about how much they've wanted to stop Elizabeth 'for years.'

The small group who left returns carrying large

clay jugs. Except for the glowing blue markings around the fattest part, the pitchers appear like any ordinary ancient bit of pottery. We're all—even me —damn thirsty, so the presence of water distracts everyone into a frenzy of drinking. Despite being about the size to hold roughly two gallons, it keeps on pouring long after they ought to have been empty.

"This is so trippy," whispers Tammy.

"Magic." Allison wags her eyebrows. "Enchanted pitchers are probably as common here as electric tea kettles back home."

"How'd they even buy them?" asks Tammy. "Do the people here take credit cards?"

"Or even speak English?" asks Anthony.

"They're not speaking any language from our world," says a blonde woman from the group who fetched water. "It shares multiple sounds with Persian, but also Czech. Can't comment on the grammar or syntax since I didn't recognize a single word."

"So… how'd you get water?" I ask.

"Lots of hand signals and pantomiming." She smiles. "And conjured gold."

"At least gold is precious here," says the man next to her.

Tammy clamps a hand over her mouth to stop from laughing. Yeah, they basically stole the water since the conjured gold will disappear in a few hours. Stealing water doesn't bother me at all, but someone's going to go on a hunt for a thief that doesn't exist.

Max returns carrying a large cloth sack. He sets it down, rummages, and hands out new clothing for everyone. Allison helps out with an illusion of a privacy curtain so we can all change. She also needs to do some magical alterations on Kingsley's garments so they fit him. Apparently, no one in this world is as beefy as him. These garments are an interesting commingling of Arabic and Roman styles. At least the tunic/dress he hands me is comfortable. Tammy ends up wearing a tunic and baggy pants that—according to Anthony—makes her look like a girl playing Aladdin in a high school play.

He should talk. He looks like a grown up playing a Hobbit.

Tammy snickers.

Allison's longer dress is somewhere between Roman senator's wife and the girl holding the wine pitcher in the background of movies about Caesar.

"All right," says Max. "You will be able to blend in now. Sam, I think it will be best for you five to scout around the city in search of Elizabeth or any sign of her people. My connection to her is far too strong for even Tammy to mask. Also, dark masters have a much easier time sensing my people. The effect will be more pronounced here in a world where magic is so much stronger."

I nod. "All right. Was feeling a bit like a fifth wheel just sitting around."

Max pulls a cheap-looking copper ring out and

hands it to me. "This will help. Wearing it will allow you to understand the spoken language of anyone you are concentrating on. Also, anything you say will be understood in a person's native language."

"Interesting." I take it, ponder a moment, then hand it to Tammy. "Better she wears it for now since she can eavesdrop on the entire city at once."

"Oh, joy." Tammy accepts the ring, smirking, but puts it on. "You're getting it back if you need to adjust anyone's brain."

"Okay."

While Max and the Light Warriors get into a discussion about reopening the interdimensional gate, my crew and I head out and make our way among the other tents. An area of open sand somewhat longer than a football field separates the innermost tent from the gate in the actual city's gigantic wall. It really is a ridiculous shape for a wall, having forty-five degree angled slopes both inside and outside the city. Anyone athletic enough could run up one side and down the other, assuming it's not enchanted to be slippery or loaded with spike traps. Considering we've seen a magical flashlight and water pitchers capable of holding far more than their size should allow, I'm going to guess the wall has some kind of defensive spell in it.

Hmm. Maybe they built it more to protect against the wind than invasion? The angle would redirect a strong breeze upward, where a flat wall might just collapse altogether. Hopefully such a sandstorm will miss us.

A group of men in black leather armor with red trim, red skirts, and sandals guarding the gate into the city all give us weird looks.

Mom! whispers Tammy in my head. *They're suspicious of us for being so pale. They've never seen white people before—except for the new empress. They think we're from 'across the great water' like her.*

Oh, shit. They would be right, of course.

I grab her hand, borrow the language ring, and hammer them over the head with a mental command to ignore we exist. I'm not surprised to find a deeper bit of mind control forcing them to be loyal to Elizabeth in there. It didn't come from her, though. I get a glimpse of a male ascendant dark master wandering among them on a battlefield in the aftermath of a skirmish. Someone, most likely Elizabeth's forces, shredded dozens of other men, who lay dead all around them. The ascendant approaches them and stares into their eyes.

It's strong, but I pluck the command loose, then make sure they don't remember seeing us go by.

The guards stand there in a stupor while we hurry through the gap in the wall, entering the city within. It's like traveling between two halves of an Egyptian pyramid after it's been cut in half. Faint echoes from inside tell me there are passageways or perhaps even rooms inside the wall itself, but no visible doors or windows can be seen. Makes sense.

The main gate would be the most defended part of the city. Kinda silly to have a door to the interior of the wall where invaders could easily reach it.

Tammy slips her finger back into the ring but keeps holding my hand.

Allison casts a spell to make us 'less noticeable' as she thinks of it. If we merely walk around and stay out of peoples' way, no one will acknowledge we exist unless they are specifically searching for us. Neat trick. If we touch someone or get close enough to breathe on them, they'll realize we exist.

We wander into a large, open square full of people, merchant wagons, a few small stages, and a fountain more intended for drinking water than being fancy. Looks like anyone's free to help themselves to water, though several enterprising people—mostly teenage boys—have set up booths to sell pitchers and cups. Unlike the other ones, these don't appear to be magic.

Tammy looks around, no doubt listening in on people's thoughts and conversations. Something makes her squeeze my hand real hard after about eight minutes, but she doesn't say anything right away. We cross the bazaar and enter a street leading into the city proper. Various shops on both sides sell all manner of trade goods from clothes to furniture to art objects, and of course, magical 'appliances.'

Curiosity gets Tammy's attention. She stares at the place, no doubt scanning the minds of those inside, then explains they sell primarily items to preserve food, store water, clean clothing, and make light… not really appliances in the sense I think of the word.

We continue walking, Tammy randomly reading minds around us, looking for general useful information as well as if anyone has seen Elizabeth. All of a sudden, she squeezes my hand real hard. Sensing my worry, she gives me an 'I wanna go home' look.

Mom, they have slaves here… and it doesn't matter like what color people are. They grab poor people, drunk people, debtors, prisoners, street orphans, anything. It's like normal for them.

I grumble in my head. Of course, my immediate first thought is going on a city-wide rampage and killing all the slave traders. Violent vigilante justice isn't a terribly noble thing, but in some cases—like slavery and anyone who'd hurt a child—I'll make exceptions. I'm still half tempted to throw Paxton's father down the stairs, but I'm resisting. Maybe I'll simply give him a memory of being thrown down the stairs if I ever meet him.

"Relax, Tam. I won't let anyone grab you or Mom," says Anthony.

Tammy laughs nervously. "I don't think Mom's gonna let anyone grab Mom."

"She is slightly more difficult to kidnap than the average woman." Kingsley gives me a little tap on the butt.

"Hah. Just a little." I narrow my eyes. "Anything else we need to know, Tammy? Is this place weird about women showing their faces in public or anything like that?"

Tammy resumes eavesdropping.

"I wouldn't think so," says Kingsley. "None of the women in sight are covering up excessively."

"No rule about that," says Tammy. "And wow, I'm kinda having trouble believing what I'm seeing in people's thoughts."

"Lemme guess," says Anthony, folding his arms. "It's men who are discriminated against here?"

Tammy shakes her head. "Nothing like that. It's this whole slavery thing. It's legal and normal here... yet they're also really progressive with women." Tammy pauses, turning and scanning minds. "Okay. I get the feeling there are social classes here, but it's based on age, wealth, and if you're a slave or not. Obviously, slaves are the bottom of the social pyramid, but... oh, that's beyond messed up."

"Do I even want to know?" I ask.

She gawks around at a few nearby people. "Umm. Like, it's a bigger crime to kill a slave than kill a free person here... because the slave is a piece of property with more monetary value. This place *really* hates thieves."

"Wow." Anthony blinks.

"Okay, I think this is how they're set up... slaves are at the bottom. Then children who have no real rights or voice. Then old people who are kinda treated with respect but are also dismissed. Like this society considers all old people cute and funny, but not to be taken seriously. Then there's normal adults, then rich adults."

"Do these differences actually mean anything to them?" asks Kingsley. "Any tangible differences in how the laws treat them?"

"Umm, I get the feeling it's mostly how people talk to each other. Not really legal differences."

"Let's just find Elizabeth, separate her head from the rest of her, and be on our way," says Kingsley.

"Umm, there's more." Tammy bites her lip. "It's about Elizabeth."

Anthony chuckles. "Shouldn't you have brought her up first? She's like our entire reason for being here."

"Kinda got distracted by being terrified we're going to be kidnapped." Tammy exhales.

"If anyone dares try, they will regret it." I glare around at random people, suddenly paranoid that slave-catchers are lurking everywhere.

"We're all at risk," says Allison. "We look like outsiders."

Anthony laughs. "I'd like to see someone try to kidnap Kingsley."

Allison snickers. "I doubt they know how to make chains here strong enough to hold him."

"They don't use chains," whispers Tammy. "Think collars with pain magic that go off if a person disobeys."

"Right. This dimension is officially on our no-visit list," I say. "Let's find the bitch and get out of here before *I* lead an insurrection."

Tammy leans against me. "You're too late. Elizabeth already did. People are thinking mostly about their new empress. She revealed herself to everyone yesterday as their new goddess-queen. They've already taken over the palace, killed the former king, and have promised this will become the capital of the greatest empire the world has ever known. A lot of citizens are scared out of their minds war is coming, but there's a stupid lot of them who think it's a great idea. They are happy this city will get bigger and richer when it's the heart of her empire. They don't care she's going to treat them like peasants as long as they're part of the awesome empire."

"So messed up," says Anthony. "She kills their king and they're okay with it?"

"Their king did legalize slavery." Allison shrugs. "I'd be okay with someone killing him, too."

"Yeah, except... Elizabeth's going to be far worse once they get to know her." I frown.

We walk along the larger streets for almost two hours, avoiding narrower alleys or thoroughfares. For a while, we leave merchant areas behind and roam among small dwellings crammed so close together it reminds me of row houses, only more medieval. The majority of the buildings appear to be made of either adobe or solid stone shaped by magic. Predictably, there isn't much wood around for building.

Here and there, we spot people—mostly boys in

their later teens—wearing gold or silver collars inscribed with glowing orange, green, or red writing. Other than their clothing appearing a little more drab than others, they don't look to be in miserable spirits or poor physical condition. Most jogged by as if on an errand, while one worked sweeping the area in front of a large shop selling clothes.

My mom instincts wanted to get involved, but I forced myself not to for two reasons. One, they appeared not to be in immediate distress, and two, as they say, starting a land war in Asia is a bad idea. More accurately, riling up the entire city for a slave revolt is the exact opposite of subtle. Elizabeth needs to go down before I make waves of any other kind here.

Hey, Mom? Tammy smiles at me. *Maybe if you free them from Elizabeth, the new king will be so happy he'll give you a reward and you can ask them to outlaw slavery.*

There's a thought. I almost add 'assuming we survive,' but, oops I did think it.

"Oh, there she is." Tammy stares off into the near distance. "Sorry if I go derpy. I'm hiding us."

Derpy is Tammy's new word for looking foolish. Lately, it's when she's using so much of her brain power, the rest of her gets neglected. Blank faces, mouth open, drool. It's why Anthony has to carry her. What wonders the internet has brought civilization, right? I never even heard the word 'derp' until I had teenagers.

Drool? Really, Mom?

I pat her on the rear end. I love you, kid.

The smell of food wafting by on the breeze enchants Kingsley and Anthony as thoroughly as a snake charmer's flute. The two guys head for a nearby place with the look of an inn or restaurant. Allison starts to follow, but stops to look back in a 'you coming' way. Oh hell. Food wouldn't be a bad idea. I escort Tammy since she's already become kinda out of it.

Five stairs lead down from the front door into a recessed tavern room. Even though I'm not being affected by the punishing heat, I can tell it's noticeably cooler inside this building than outside. Since my daughter is zoned, I take the translation ring. While the others sit at a round table in the back corner, I prowl the room in search of a 'patron.'

Because stealing is apparently the greatest crime imaginable to this society, it's time for a little generosity. A guy wearing a few gold rings and ruby earrings stands out as 'probably rich' to me. This goes against most of who I am, but it's getting chalked up to the greater good of stopping Elizabeth. If we starve, we won't have the strength to stop her. Also, we don't have the time to run around doing odd jobs for people to earn some money.

I approach the rich guy's table. He's sitting with two people. One's a slender young woman who's probably in her early twenties, dressed in fine, almost-transparent silks dyed cyan and violet as well as a silver slave collar. Her demeanor and body language reminds me of a personal assistant for a demanding boss who also has the ability to command her to sleep with him whenever he wants. Hates her job but can't quit.

The rich guy's other friend is a man in his thirties. I assume he's definitely some kind of bodyguard due to his big muscles, scars and the large sword strapped across his back.

Rich dude's teasing forty but might not be there yet. Long beard, lots of rings and jewelry. Some grey in his beard.

I eye the clearly beaten-down slave girl. Okay, my regret at basically stealing from this guy is gone.

Approaching the table, I dive into the bodyguard's mind and implant the sudden, powerful sensation that he's about to experience explosive diarrhea. No, it's not going to cause him to actually blow up 'down below,' but it will send him sprinting off for the nearest... whatever this place has equivalent to toilets.

The rich guy jumps at his guard's abrupt departure, calling, "Nasi? Where are you going?"

I stare at the rich guy until he makes eye contact, and jump into his brain next. He's pretty weak-willed. Good. It only takes me a minute to do a little brain surgery on him. In his memory, he now believes that as Nasi rushed to the bathroom, an assassin tried to kill him. Safa, his slave girl, threw herself in the way, delaying the attacker long enough for a good Samaritan—me—to chase the assassin off after defeating him in a brief sword fight. He is going to reward me with fifty or so of those lahz coins and reward Safa by giving her freedom.

He stares into space, briefly lost in a mental fog.

I look at the woman and go into her head. It's safer for her if she believes the story as truth, too. Since I get the distinct feeling this girl would *not* have risked herself to save him, I give her the believable alteration that he threw her in the way of the assassin. It might catch her off guard when the guy rewards her for saving him, even if she believes he used her as a body-shield, but it's extremely doubtful she'll protest.

The man fishes out a handful of coins and hands them to me. A false memory of him profusely thanking me beats his making a scene in the inn. I send him on his way to deal with whatever legal process is required to give the young woman her freedom, then head back to our table.

Takes a little bit of brain poking before I realize things are somewhat different here. As in, this world has no table servers. We have to go up to the bar and order food, then carry it back ourselves. Not a big deal. The food is similar to Tandoori grilled chicken, sausage, and something else, probably goat or maybe camel. Thus far, animals here are basically the same as our Earth. All of us eating— including Kingsley having his fill and Anthony eating enough for three—resulted in me spending three coins and getting back thirteen smaller, thinner bronze coins as change.

Curious, I dive into the bartender's mind and probe his understanding of money. One lahz is about the same as a $20 bill. The bronze coins, simply called 'ra,' are close to dollar bills. Basically, our dinner cost $47. We have just over $100 left. To the owner of the tavern, we're big spenders. This place isn't expensive, but Kingsley's and Anthony's appetites are already the stuff of legend.

I pocket the coins and head back to the table. Tammy is still eating since her focus on hiding us slows her down.

And yeah, it looks like my mission objective might have expanded a bit.

Yes, we're still after Elizabeth and her merry band of psychopaths.

But this slavery business doesn't sit well with me.

No, not at all.

Chapter Four
A New Immortal

Once we're done eating, we resume searching the city.

At least now we have Tammy as sort of a compass. If we travel in a particular direction for a while and she gets more mannequin-like, it's a good sign we're heading toward Elizabeth. Honestly, it's not necessary to use my daughter as a human dowsing rod. I'm ninety-nine percent certain the bitch is going to be taking up residence in the former king's castle.

If it wasn't broad daylight, I'd fly straight up for an aerial view of the city.

Allison thinks, *Hang on, I got it*, then raises her hand. She casts a spell, throwing a peanut-sized spot of yellow light into the air. Thanks to our mental link, I get to see what she sees: it's as if her eyes popped out and went zooming toward the sky.

From the air, the city we're in resembles a gigantic twelve-pointed Chinese throwing star around a shimmering blue lake. It has to be some manner of spring or oasis, a water source. Twelve canals run outward from the lake, in line with the 'points' on the outer wall. Darn good explanation for how a city this big cropped up in the middle of the desert. Also looks like despite their extreme fixation on money and hate of thievery, water is completely free to any who want it.

Guess dehydrated people don't pay taxes or join the army, right?

On the northeastern shore of the giant lake stands a tall pyramid-shaped castle. At least, I'm assuming it's a castle given the fancy stairs on the north side and palace guards. I imagine the Great Pyramids of Egypt once looked like this, being all smooth and shiny white. This castle has two main differences from those, however. The top isn't pointy, but flat, like someone chopped off the uppermost twelve feet of an eight-story pyramid. Second difference is the presence of numerous patios and windows around the outer face. It's definitely being used as a building and not as a tomb.

The resemblance to pyramids in our world both with the castle and city wall is uncanny. Though, I suppose a pyramid might simply be the most efficient way to stack a crapload of rock. Allison's spell gives a decent sense of 'you are here,' so we both have a general idea of which way we need to go to reach the palace at the edge of the lake.

We're not planning to do anything yet beyond verify Elizabeth is here. Yeah, I know. We've essentially done that already, but I'd like to get a look at the castle up close... and get a lay of the land, so to speak.

Allison releases the seeing spell and our vision returns to normal.

We navigate a handful of streets, passing residences as well as another merchant district—damn this city is huge—on our way to the middle. Mostly, I'm trying to go west to the nearest canal and follow it in a straight line to the central lake, since the streets are quite winding and maze-like.

Our express trip to the city center takes a momentary detour when I spot a stage set up at the end of an alley, surrounded on three sides by high walls. Only, the people on it aren't doing a theater production… it's a slave market.

Ah, hell.

Three young men are being sold, likely as laborers. A row of prison cells against the right wall holds three more as well as a pair of young women. None of the people in the cells have collars. One woman and two of the men in the cell are bound with ropes. I can't help myself and look at their thoughts. As Tammy feared, the three who are tied have recently been grabbed off the street since they had no family to claim them and can't prove they don't belong enslaved. The ones in the cells are locked up awaiting collars. All are debating their odds of escaping.

Allison whispers to Kingsley and Anthony what's on my mind, namely, storming over there and raiding the slave market. She puts a hand on my shoulder as if to hold me back.

"Sam, it's the society here. This is their normal."

I exhale hard. "Normal doesn't mean it's right."

"Yeah, I'm with you there," says Allison, "but if we attack them, *we'll* be the outlaws. If we kick the hornet's nest here, we might not be able to blindside Elizabeth unaware. Right now, she thinks she's untouchable. We have to catch her by surprise and do whatever we're going to do before she can mount a defense. It's the only chance we have."

Agreeing with her boils my blood, but it makes sense. What's happening here to those people would have been going on anyway, even if Elizabeth hadn't come here. I'd never have even known about it. And, thus far, from what we've mined out of people's heads, slaves aren't *too* bad off. It's not like the American South where they whipped people mercilessly. More like how Ancient Rome regarded 'slave' as a low social rank.

In more of a hurry than ever, I storm off down the street. Anthony, carrying his sister, jogs after me while Kingsley hovers protectively close to Allison. She is thrilled. He knows she has an innocent crush on him and likes to mess with her.

The canal is bigger than I expected based on the aerial view. It's as wide as a four-lane highway, but shallow. We walk through a crowd of children, some playing, some apparently working as runners fetching water. Fortunately, none of them have slave collars or I'm not sure I'd have been able to hold myself back. Their thoughts confirm they're voluntarily working as water runners to help their families afford food.

A few people swim, which kinda makes me squirm at the thought they drink the same water.

Whatever. We hopefully won't be here long enough to worry about it. Allison senses a surprisingly strong outward current in the canal and believes it's being moved along by magic. Not sure how that helps protect against bacteria, but at least it's not stagnant.

We follow the canal for about a mile and three quarters before the central lake—and castle—come into view. The area around the lake is awash in lush vegetation, mostly grass and palm trees, but also several types of flowers and some unfamiliar bushes taller than me. It is *really* weird to be wearing clothes like I'm about to participate in a theater production of the story of Julius Caesar's assassination while walking through knee-high grass around a desert oasis. I realize we've gone to an alternate world, but the feeling of having gone back in time, too, is eerily strong.

"It's because you haven't heard a single airplane, car, helicopter, or radio since we arrived," says Allison.

"What?" Kingsley glances over at us.

"She's thinking it feels like we went back in time."

"We kinda did." Anthony points at the pyramid castle. "Elizabeth's in there."

"How can you tell?" asks Allison.

"I dunno. Just kinda know. Oh, and Tammy has devolved into a gummi bear."

"She what?" I spin, alarmed.

My daughter is limp in his arms, like she passed out drunk. Except her eyes are open and full of awareness, as well as a sense of grim determination. She's all brain and no body at this point, doing all she can to shield us.

I quickly lead us around the lakeshore to the huge street running past the north face of the castle. A massive courtyard spreads out just beyond the main palace entrance. It's mostly empty at the moment except for a partially smashed statue of, I assume, the former king. Multiple huge buildings surrounding the square look like mansions belonging to nobility or perhaps temples to whatever gods they have here.

Beyond the courtyard is the palace itself. Broad stairs lead up two full stories to an extended platform sheltered under a stone arch supported by eight columns carved to resemble serpentine dragons. Recent bloodstains are everywhere on the steps and the area near their base. The tattered remains of decorative banners still hang from rings along both sides of the canopy. Elizabeth's people tore down the prior king's crest, apparently.

I'm shocked to see only two palace guards standing at the midway point of the stairs. Both wear the same black leather armor as the men stationed at the city gates. These two look notice-ably beefier, like they've had access to a modern gym—and steroids. I start peeking at the mind of the one on the left, but awareness of being spied on appears in his outermost thoughts. Whoops! I drop the connection as fast as my brain can react, hopefully before he realized where—and who—I am.

The guy doesn't look like a vampire. He's standing out in the blistering sun, and there isn't a single wisp of smoke around him. It's highly unlikely anyone in this timeline has invented sun-block, nor does he appear to be slathered in it. He *is* sweating, but nowhere near as much as I would be if I stood around wearing black armor in 108 degree heat—even if it's 'light armor' like the kind the Roman Centurions wore, complete with a skirt and such. But it's still armor. And black. What kind of moron wears black in the desert?

"The guards might be paranormal," I say. "What, exactly, I'm not sure."

Kingsley sniffs the air, narrows his eyes. "Hmm. They still smell like mortals, but feel supernatural."

"We can probably—oh, whoa. Incoming," whis-pers Anthony. He pivots, using Tammy's limp body like a mannequin to point down the street.

Amid the back-and-forth foot traffic, a group of about twenty men trying too hard to look casual moves in the direction of the castle. They've all got dingy whitish-beige cloaks on over armor mostly in the same style as the palace guards, only plain leathery brown.

"They're going to rush the palace," I say.

"Read their minds?" asks Anthony.

"No. It's obvious merely from looking at them… but…" I stare at the lead man and try to get a read on his thoughts.

Sure enough, he's mortal and the door to his mind is wide open. They're the former king's soldiers, some of about a thousand who escaped alive and went into hiding. He has no idea what kind of monsters they're dealing with, but he suspects the invaders are weak in the day, so they hope an attack during sunlight will let them retake the castle.

When the group nears the base of the steps, they throw off their dingy cloaks, draw falchion-style swords, and rush up at the two palace guards. They, too, draw swords. Before the question 'should we get involved' can even form in my brain, four soldiers are dead. The palace guards run through the attackers like they're running through a field slicing down bamboo poles incapable of fighting back. All twenty-one humans are dead or mortally wounded in under a minute.

"Ack." Allison covers her mouth. "I was going to ask if we should help."

"Bit late," deadpans Kingsley.

"We can take these punks." Anthony looks around. "Where should I put Tam?"

I study the palace guards' motions as they examine the bodies, all of which rolled down the angled castle wall, slid, or were kicked to the ground at the base of the steps. These two men didn't look faster than me or even particularly skilled at swordsmanship. Then again, the humans put up little in the way of a defense. Vampiric speed could allow anyone to kill ordinary people quite easily using a sword. My son's likely correct. I could take one of these guys out and not stress too bad over it. Two on one and I'm not as confident of winning. But me, Kingsley, Allison, *and* Anthony on two of these guys? Yeah, we'd mop them up.

They certainly didn't look as fast as the ascendant dark masters, and they don't appear to be vampires.

Question is, what the hell are they?

Guys, says Tammy in a weak mental voice. *The frontal approach isn't going to work.*

"We can take 'em," says Anthony.

It's not those two you should be worrying about. It's the other fifty or so inside.

Anthony leans back. "Oh… good point."

Grr. I'm not helpless, Anthony!

"Huh?" I ask.

Ant. He's being a dumbass. He's still willing to charge right in the front door, but he's afraid of me *getting hurt out here.*

I pat her on the head. "Hon, you're not helpless, but you also aren't superhuman."

It's fairly unlikely one of them would attack

Tammy, since she's both unarmed and wouldn't be participating in any fighting—except possibly humming Justin Bieber music into people's heads to distract them.

Grr. I hate feeling so useless.

Aww, hon. You are absolutely *not* useless. The guys who invented the first atomic bombs couldn't beat a soldier in a fistfight, but they ended the damn war.

My daughter sighs mentally. *Those men helped the government murder thousands of innocent civilians. Bombing entire cities like that is horrible and evil.*

Okay, okay. Bad analogy. Umm, you're like the people at mission control coordinating everything. You're the most valuable part of our team. Because of you, Elizabeth doesn't know we're here yet. And… we also effectively have radio communication in a time without electricity.

"They might have magic radios," whispers Allison, listening in our conversation. "I mean, we found a weird flashlight."

It's okay, Mom. I know what you meant. Oh, Max wants us to come back to, umm, the base tent.

"Not a bad idea." Kingsley looks around. "We're growing obvious standing here watching the slaughter without running and screaming like everyone else."

Allison glances at him. "My spell is still hiding us as long as we don't get too close."

"Still." I hold my arms out. "Let's go back to

the tent."

Everyone grabs on, and I summon the dancing flame.

Chapter Five
Resistance

The interior of Max's tent appears in the flickering flame.

I beckon it closer and closer until it expands into the size of a yawning portal and passes around us. Our surroundings shift in an instant. Several Light Warriors jump in surprise at our sudden appearance. Tammy snaps out of her paralyzed state but seems content to remain draped in her brother's arms. She looks exhausted. The fragrance of various foods and spices hang in the air. Damn. Now I've got a craving for Indian. Big time. Or Thai. Dammit. I can't tell what it smells more like between Indian or Thai.

Moroccan? asks Allison.

I blink at her. No idea. Never had it.

"Ahh, Sam…" Max walks up to me, smiling. "Tammy has shared with me already the details of your reconnaissance mission."

"Good. Do you have any idea what the heck those two palace guards are?" I ask.

"As a matter of fact, I do. Elizabeth used the same trick in the last months of the war. They are dark masters who have established an impermanent binding to a still-living human."

Kingsley whistles. "How dangerous are they?"

"Not terribly." Max shrugs. "They are strong and fast, yes, but lack the resilience or regeneration of vampires. There is no need to use silver weapons on them as they die as easily as the living. No mental powers, claws, fangs, or anything of the sort."

"So basically, Captain America, but a bad guy?" says Anthony.

"Say what?" I ask.

Anthony flexes. "Comic books, Ma. The government took a normal dude and made him superhumanly strong and tough, but not as much as Superman. Cap is still mortal."

"Super soldiers, basically," says Kingsley.

"Yes. But they shouldn't be too difficult for you or Sam to take on... or the Fire Warrior." Max winks, then shifts his attention to a man with long black hair and a tall face, a man who wasn't here before. "Everyone, this is Mardat."

Mardat bows in greeting. He's somewhere between twenty and forty and looks more or less like an ordinary citizen, except for the confidence in his eyes and his posture. This man is nowhere near as relaxed or ordinary as he appears to be. He's not giving off aggression, more a sense he's hyper aware of everyone around him. The read I get from his outermost thoughts confirms my suspicion... he's a spy.

"Our arrival here has not gone unnoticed, apparently," says Max. "Fortunately, Mardat's people—and not Elizabeth's arc the ones who realized we are not locals."

"Sorry," says Madelyn Singleton, one of the mystics who initially went out to get water. "Probably dumb of the conspicuous blonde to go looking for something to drink."

The Light Warriors chuckle.

Max waves at her in a 'don't worry about it' way, then looks back to me. "Mardat was part of the former king's military and spy network. One of the few relatively senior people left alive."

I raise both eyebrows, pretending to be surprised. "Spy network? There's nothing but desert for miles in every direction. Who, exactly, are they spying on?"

Mardat clasps his hands in front of himself. "Much of our work occurred within the capital city. There are four other kingdoms bordering ours, and six smaller cities in our territory. All of which are several days' travel by camel, or one day by sail."

"Sail?" asks Tammy.

"We occasionally use wind-powered wagons. They are, as you may expect, dependent on the weather. With a good strong wind, we can cover great distances at high speed."

I'm thinking something like wheeled sailboats. Okay, makes sense. Probably means I could fly there in a couple hours, then.

"If there's a need to send word to other cities, I can cover distance quite fast," I say.

Mardat purses his lips in thought. "We do not think the empress has gone outside the walls of Iskariya yet. She will certainly become aware we plot against her if the other garrisons return to the capital."

Max gestures at us. "Please, tell them what you told me, Mardat."

"Of course," says Mardat, nodding. "Our seers have predicted the new empress will be terrible and cruel."

"We suspected that," I say. "It's kinda why we're here."

"Interestingly, they said we will receive help from afar, but it shall not cross the deserts of Mishennadi."

"Sorry... not following."

He grins at me. "It means our aid will come from quite far away, but will not traverse the great sands separating us from the rest of the continent. Outsiders who somehow arrive in Iskariya without needing to cross the vast desert around it."

"Basically us, Ma," says Anthony.

"Indeed." Max pats my son on the shoulder. "We believe the vision indicates that sending word to the outlying cities to request aid will alert Elizabeth to danger and complicate our efforts."

Kingsley holds up a hand. "Are we really going to base our plans on someone having visions?"

"This world is not exactly like ours," says Max. "There are many small differences, many of the magical variety. We are working as fast as we can to bring in additional Light Warriors. The luxury of time is not one we have. For each hour Elizabeth remains here, the more powerful she will become. She will eventually grow strong enough to conquer more than the City of Iskariya, and with every new city and territory her army occupies, her power will grow. Eventually, she will reach a point where we can no longer pose any threat to her."

"She's still only one person," I say.

"I'm not merely speaking in terms of political or military power." Max glances sideways at the mystics among his people, who are conferring in the back of the tent. "The magic of this world is prevalent to the point she can draw upon the fear of mortals."

"What the hell does that mean?" I ask.

"It means, as more and more come to fear her, the more powerful she becomes. The fear itself will galvanize her magic."

"Great."

The Alchemist nods gravely. "As more fall under her dominion, she will eventually reach the point of becoming akin to a demigod."

"How long do we have?" asks Allison.

"Hmm." Max shifts his jaw side to side while pondering. "I am perhaps overstating the urgency for motivation. The sooner we confront her, the easier it will be. While it is true each hour she remains here may complicate our task, we most likely have between eighteen months to two years before she becomes so powerful we have no chance of defeating her. However, I was rather hoping to be home in time to catch Conan."

"The barbarian?" asks Anthony.

Max chuckles. "No, the comedian."

I'd laugh, but… yeah. Things are a little on the heavy side at the moment. "You really think this could be over in a few hours?"

"I do. I am trying to stay positive." Max smiles, then waves for everyone to gather close. "Let us go over what we know and establish a strategy."

Madelyn walks over to stand beside us along with Yasmeen and Olivia. Kingsley, Allison, and I, plus Mardat and the big warrior Anthony's been talking to—Dillon Hewitt—form a circle a bit like the Round Table of Camelot… only with less armor and no table.

Anthony and Tammy back up to let more of the experienced Light Warriors closer.

Our discussion starts off with me describing the palace guards having superhuman agility and strength. Mardat appears visibly shaken upon learning they slaughtered so many of the old king's soldiers in under a minute. Max assures him we have means of dealing with such beings and not to lose hope. The former spy—I say 'former' because he's no longer officially employed by the royalty here—goes over possible ways to infiltrate the castle. Our best option sounds like a water tunnel on the south face of the castle. It's not a sewer, rather an inlet from the lake supplying the castle's plumbing. Surprisingly, they have faucets and such here. Water is drawn in via enchanted pipes, so there is no need for pumps.

"The only complication with the pipe," says Mardat, "is the grating on the end isn't designed to be opened. It is mortared in place."

Kingsley cracks his knuckles. "Designs can be modified."

While Mardat sketches out a basic illustration of a seriously heavy metal grid, I'm about to ask how we're all able to understand him, but Tammy telepathically informs me Yasmeen cast a spell on him using the same magic Max embedded in the rings.

"And if he can't break it open, I can get us past it," I say. "Speaking of which, do you have access to any realistic paintings of an interior room of the castle? A good enough mental picture will allow me to teleport a small group in."

Mardat contemplates the idea for a moment before shaking his head. "The castle is heavily patrolled. Unless you have a way to be certain you will not appear and be noticed immediately, it would be best to take your time going in. Also, Safihr, King Wareem's chief magister, placed numerous defensive spells on the castle to prevent magical intrusion."

"Hmm. I'm not sure what Samantha does is considered magic," says Yasmeen.

I chuckle. "Not sure it isn't. Can science explain teleportation?"

Most everyone makes 'she kinda has a point' face, except for Max who covers his mouth to hold in a chuckle—and Mardat who appears confused by the word 'science.' From there, Max suggests splitting our efforts into me leading a small team into the castle via the pipe while he and the rest of the Light Warriors gear up for a frontal assault. The idea being, we get into position to surprise Elizabeth from behind while she's distracted dealing with the main attack. Considering it will take us a little while to make it into the castle, they're going to work on opening another interdimensional portal to bring in the rest of the Light Warriors.

One downside of being an esoteric order of supernatural guardians is there aren't too many of them. Max expects to have a force of about fifty or so, and this is after he pulls them in from multiple lodges around the globe. Italy, for example, only has four Light Warriors.

My 'insertion team' is going to consist of me, Kingsley, and Allison. Anthony will stay here in the tent as an honorary—and perhaps permanent based on the way he's been looking at them—Light Warrior. They seem to be counting on him as the bulwark of their front line when they decide to make their move, but for now, they want him to stay out of sight at the tent. It is definitely a weird feeling to have grown adults suggesting my son is a source of strength and courage for them. Sure, the Fire Warrior is huge, strong, and tough... but my boy is still a boy.

It's fine, Mom, says Tammy. *It'll be the Fire Warrior taking the beating, not Ant. That guy is way over eighteen.*

I exhale.

Tammy will remain at the tent, even after Anthony and the others launch their assault on the castle. She will concentrate on shielding everyone's mind from detection and mind-control. Having her focus on defense is sorta like a bulletproof vest for the brain. Not a guaranteed resistance to a vampire's mental powers, but she will definitely tilt the odds in the Light Warriors' favor.

While the three of us move into position at the castle, Max and his people plan to travel far enough out into the desert away from the City of Iskariya so the portal won't be visible. Since this dimension is so much more magical than Earth, such portals don't need to rely on ley line intersections to provide a massive power boost. Here, they can open an interdimensional portal almost anywhere. Still, the doorways are huge, bright, and obvious. If any of Elizabeth's minions see it, she will know we're coming.

Max is certain any chance we have at victory requires he bring in as many Light Warriors and other potential allies as possible. Don't ask me how he's communicating with them between dimensions, but a small army has gathered, ready to go as soon as he opens the gate for them.

Thanks to my daughter, everyone in this dimension will stay in contact so we know what's going on.

"This goes without saying, though I am almost loathe to suggest it." Max bows his head, pausing a moment. "If you have the opportunity to cleanly assassinate her, you should take it. The loss of her leadership will strike a morale blow to the others and make our jobs much easier."

"You plan to wipe out *all* the dark masters here?" asks Allison.

"Such a thing would be ideal, but I fear… impossible. *If* we gain the upper hand, as soon as they realize they are losing, they will abandon her cause. Without her leadership, it is unlikely they will remain focused on conquest. dark masters are, by nature, somewhat solitary beings. Eliminate her influence, and they will most likely scatter. Of course, it means this world will develop a limited number of creatures like vampires and werewolves, but there are already beasts here far worse. The effect will be relatively minimal."

"Where would a dark master go if the host is destroyed?" I ask. "The Void is gone."

"What about the ascendant ones?" asks Tammy.

Max holds his hands up as if our barrage of questions rained on him like arrows. "There are precious few ways to destroy a dark master permanently. Sam, you carry one… the Devil Killer. I have access to another, but it requires entrapping them in an enchanted vessel and then performing several hours of rituals. Such a process destroys them one at a time and is hardly efficient for warfare. Also, I left the vase at home."

Anthony chuckles. "Ma, did you turn off the coffee maker?"

I wink. "Great. Something else to worry about."

"You are correct in saying The Void is gone." Max nods at me. "However, it would have been irrelevant since it belongs to our dimension. As soon as they came to this world, they would not have been bound to the Void we made in ours so long ago. Unbound dark masters will do here what they did prior to our creating their prison: they will appear as shadow figures, haunts, or ghosts... until they find another host."

"There's also no delay between hosts," says Anthony. "When the Void existed, if someone put a silver bolt in a vampire's heart, the dark master would get thrown back down to the Void and be stuck there for a long time before they could get into another host. Now, they could jump into anyone close to death as soon as they wanted to. Kinda like what pops did to the other sick Anthony."

"Very good." Max smiles at him.

My son gets that awkward-proud look to him, like he's grateful for the praise but ashamed of something. Probably because he learned about dark masters from Danny.

"The boy is right," says Olivia. "In the time before our predecessors created the Void, vampires would spring right back up after being destroyed—in an entirely different body. This, as you might expect, made them extremely difficult to track. The Void is the reason humanity has not known of large armies of vampires roving the countryside. It takes them so long to return, they have become relegated to myths."

"Used to," whispers Allison. "Someone left the water on in the bathtub and the Void got condemned. So to speak."

"Aye." Max grumbles. "We'll need to see about recreating one after this is all over."

Murmurs of agreement go around the room.

"What if she's too powerful already?" asks Kingsley.

"I have to believe we got here in time," says Max. "Remember, we're not relying on the three of you defeating her all by yourselves. Ideally, you will wait for us to begin the attack on the front door. When she is distracted managing our assault, you strike from behind. If you do make a move before us, and it does not go well, do your best to keep her busy long enough for us to get there."

"Isn't the whole point to kill her?" Allison winces. "Sorry, I know she's your mother and all, but…"

"It is fine." Max waves dismissively. "The woman you know as Elizabeth ceased being my mother many, many lifetimes ago. If you can put an

VAMPIRE EMPRESS

end to her, do so. I am merely saying you should know we will be there as soon as possible to back you up."

I nod. "All right. So when are we getting started?"

Max looks at his wrist, checking a watch he's not wearing. "Well, Conan's on in four hours."

No one thinks he's serious about wanting to be back in our world in time for a late show, but message received. He wants to move as fast as possible.

I hug my kids together. "You guys please be careful."

"I will, Ma," says Anthony.

"Yeah. I'll just hide in the tent." Tammy fidgets, looking simultaneously relieved and ashamed of herself.

"You're not a chicken." I pat her on the back.

"I know. Just kinda feel like one sitting here while everyone else is busting their ass."

"Did you *see* yourself after we got out of the city?" Anthony makes zombie arms. "Blocking Elizabeth is tough. You're working harder and longer than the rest of us. The fighting will only take minutes. Meanwhile, you're here running a dang marathon."

Tammy smiles. "You can be sweet sometimes.'

"Yeah, well. Don't get used to it." He playfully punches her in the shoulder.

She hugs me again, hesitant to let go. She's still a bit clingy from her experience, seeing an alternate

75

version of herself gone totally off the deep end. Honestly, what she showed me of that version of Tammy hurt me, too. I think we're both going to be a little overprotective of each other for a while until the memory dulls. She finally releases me.

I face Kingsley and Allison. "You two ready?"

Allie looks herself over. "As ready as I'm going to be."

Kingsley rolls his head around, stretching his neck. A few of the Light Warriors cringe at the crunching. "About time. Getting bored standing around."

"All right, everyone," says Max. "Let's get to work."

Chapter Six
The Quiet Way

According to Kingsley, there are two ways to 'do war.'

In my opinion, there's quite a bunch more than simply two, but he's boiled it down to 'ways that make noise' and 'ways that don't.' Noisy war includes everything from gunfire to dropping nuclear weapons.

Less noisy war ranges from poisonings to politics. Sneaking into a castle to stab the king or queen in their sleep, for example. Or dropping radioactive polonium in a guy's tea. We're a little short on polonium, and I'm not sure it would bother Elizabeth, anyway. Trying to poison her would be about as dumb as someone expecting lava to kill the Fire Warrior.

We make our way back into the city. Tammy's mental shield is noticeable as a slight dulling of my telepathic abilities. I really have to work to figure out what people are thinking while she is concentrating on it. For the purposes of this mission, I'm still wearing Max's second translation ring. He gave Tammy the other one.

Once we're through the city gate, we head left to the nearest canal, about a quarter-mile away. The designers who made the city were wise enough to not have a canal leading straight from the entry gate to the palace's back yard. Be dumb to give an invading army a clear, unobstructed path. Thanks to Allison re-casting the spell to keep us hidden from casual observation, we make it to the canal unnoticed, despite walking past a few groups of patrolling soldiers.

They're not much of a threat, being normal humans. Still, we have no reason to hurt people merely for being victims of Elizabeth's mind-control. In the heat of a battle where it's impossible to undo the mental conditioning and they're running at me with a sword, different story.

Upon reaching the end of the canal, where it forms a round pool about twenty-five feet across, we turn right and follow it toward the city's heart. It's late afternoon now. Loads of people come and go from the various streets and alleys into the open areas along the canal. A few merchants have wagons set up from which they sell merchandise, even 'street food.' Nearly all the buildings facing the canal are shops or taverns of the more expensive-looking variety.

It takes us more than an hour to walk the full length of the canal to the city center, the city's *that* damn big. The distance between the outer wall and castle has to be over four miles. We see more soldiers on the way, though they act pretty much like ordinary cops on foot patrol.

The shore at the south edge of Lake Iskar is a veritable beach resort. Considering all the Egyptian-slash-Arabic vibes going around the place, it surprises me to see the locals wearing their birthday suits to go swimming. Yeah, I know. Dumb of me to apply any knowledge of Earth cultures here.

We make our way past the crowd, sticking to the outside while circling the lake toward the castle on the distant north shore. Lake Iskar has a generally bowl-shaped bottom, becoming gradually deeper toward the center, where a huge hole—like the drain of a massive sink—opens into a vertical shaft tinged in shades of blue, green and yellow, probably algae. Subtle ripples on the surface suggest the water is welling up from below, filling the lake continuously as the canals drain it off to the smaller pools at the ends.

That's a damn lot of water for a natural spring to be producing. Gotta be magic involved here. I'm not sure what it is about seeing an enormous opening on the bottom of a lake like this, but I can fly and it's *still* giving me vertigo, like going swimming in this lake will result in me being sucked down into the depths.

Still, it's breathtakingly beautiful. Maybe if I

survive this mess, I'll take some pictures before we leave. Of course, no one in our world would believe the pics are anything but computer-generated artwork.

We follow the shore around in a circle, stopping once we reach a waist-high wall blocking off the area between the castle and the lake, sort of an epic back yard. It's pretty obvious no one is supposed to go back there unless they're part of the castle staff or royals. Wonder how close they tolerate people swimming? Although I don't see anyone patrolling the beach inside the private area, it's unlikely they'd react favorably to ordinary people getting too close to the castle.

From here, I can kind of make out a whitish spot in the water where a pipe juts into the lake. Our way in. Unfortunately, it is completely underwater. Given the size of the land behind the castle to the lake, we're looking at traveling at least a hundred-yard distance while submerged.

Allison's not worried. She's got a breath-holding spell. Wow, you know... I think I might actually need such a spell. Haven't tried holding my breath to see what happens. Stands to reason if my body requires food, it's going to disapprove of being deprived of air for too long. Granted, the worst thing likely to happen to me from suffocation is remaining unconscious until there is air again. Still, don't want to pass out.

Kingsley nudges me. When I look up at him, he nods toward the castle, indicating a patio three stories up, where a handful of soldiers stand guard. Considering the angled walls of the pyramid, one might think we could totally run up to one of those balconies, but according to Mardat, there are defensive spells in place. Anyone trying to run up the castle walls will find themselves magically paralyzed for an hour or so. Easy for the castle guards to collect any would-be thieves, assassins, or misbehaving kids.

I mean, seriously. You don't build a giant pyramid and expect small boys *not* to dare each other to run up the side.

However, considering the former king is gone, replaced by Elizabeth, this castle has become a giant bug-zapper for humans. Anyone they find helpless on the ground is most likely volunteering to become vampire nom-noms. Or maybe a new vampire recruit.

"Wait," whispers Allison.

Kingsley and I pause to look at her.

"My spell is probably not going to stop them from seeing us since they are paying attention to watching the back of the castle. They aren't looking for us specifically, but they *are* looking for anyone in the area."

"And the water's too perfect and clear for us to hide in the lake," I say.

Allison taps her foot. "Magic is stronger in this world, right? I wonder if a conundrum jinx would work."

Thanks to our mind link, I know she's talking

about a minor hex that sets off an irresistible idea in a target's mind. Ever think of someone you saw in a movie once, but can't recall the actor's name? The same sensation eating at you until you finally remember or look it up on Google? Yeah, this hex causes a similar feeling, only instead of coming up with the name of a famous face, it's more like trying to remember the answer to the question 'what is six plus orange?'

The spell overcomes the victim with an insatiable need to figure out the answer to a question that doesn't exist. It stands a good chance of distracting them enough for us to slip by.

With that decided, Allison casts the conundrum jinx on the visible soldiers, who all suddenly make 'dammit, what was that actor's name?' face in response.

Heh. They're probably trying to figure out the square root of blueberry.

We hop the wall into the royal back yard. The soldiers don't pay attention to us, too busy making constipated, confused faces. One guy balls his fists. I've seen that expression before. Right now, his mind voice is shouting, 'dammit, *argh*, I know this!'

"Hop on my back." Kingsley hastily strips off his thawb and shifts into wolf form.

I gather the garment and jump on him.

Allison and I ride the big wolf like a horse across the sand bordering the lake. The genius of his plan becomes obvious right away—he's erasing his footprints by swishing his tail. Even if he misses one, a soldier finding animal tracks in the sand isn't going to stir up anywhere near the same kind of alarm as human footprints. They're probably going to freak out over a giant wolf print, but it won't get them searching the castle for spies.

Good boy!

Allison buries her face in his fur to mute her laughter.

Kingsley emits a playfully annoyed groan. He's assuming, based on her laughing for no reason, I thought something teasing about him. Sometimes he assumes incorrectly, but this time, he got me. He hurries across the lakeshore to a spot near the pipe.

Crap. I still have my phone on me.

"Give," says Allison. "Waterproof bag."

I fish my phone out and hand it to her. She drops it in her purse. While it's open, I stuff Kingsley's thawb in there, too.

We slip into the water, which is neither warm nor cool. Allison enchants us with a spell so we can hold our breath for fifteen minutes. She can't help but think to herself—and me by proxy—the reason she thought of such a spell was to endure being around Anthony.

Don't do that! yells Tammy in our minds. *You almost made me laugh and lose concentration.*

I duck underwater into a surreal world of bright blue. Considering how clear the water is, the sand itself here might actually *be* pale blue. Or maybe I'm seeing the light glowing out from the giant hole in the center of the lake. I feel a bit like a mouse someone dropped in a toilet bowl, really hoping no one hits the flush lever. The 'drain' is kinda scary. My fear of being 'inhaled' by it is unfounded; after all, there's definitely a current flowing *out* of the hole.

At least being underwater, we're hidden from the castle guards. I dive toward the end of a white stone pipe sticking horizontally out of the ground, far enough beneath the surface for a person to stand on top of without their head above water. A stiff current pulls on me once I get close to the end, though it's not difficult to grab the side of the stone tube and stop myself from being sucked face first into the metal grate at the end. The pipe's four-feet across. Plenty of room for us to fit. The three-inch squares in the grating, however, are going to hurt.

Algae and long plant threads coat the metal. Long diaphanous strands of vegetation flutter inward like yarn tied to a fan. It's eerie to exper-ience a current like this and be in total silence, no audible sense of an operating pump.

Kingsley shifts back to human form, then swims around in front of the pipe. Yeah, he's butt naked. He grabs the grating in both hands. His long hair trails forward, drawn inward by the moving water. After a moment of examining the grate, he braces his feet on the lakebed and gives a sharp tug.

Stone gives way with a sharp *crack* I feel in my bones—a weird effect from being underwater.

He pulls the grating out of the pipe end, clearing

the way for me and Allison to let the current sweep us into it. Kingsley backs into the pipe, pulling the grating back into place. Looks like he didn't smash it to the point it won't stay put. Maybe the water flow is holding it in place.

The three of us tuck our arms to our sides, now 'flying' down a round passage of relatively clean white stone. The water's moving too much for any algae to gather on the inside.

Once again, I absolutely adore being me. As in, a vampire with night vision eyes. Otherwise, this pitch-dark tube would terrify me. Bad enough being completely submerged inside a water-filled pipe. Talk about nightmare fuel. That *plus* not being able to see anything would be horrifying.

We cruise along at a speed similar to a brisk walk if we float idle, but I'm in a hurry. Never been claustrophobic in my life, but this is tweaking a nerve, so I try to swim faster. Every thirty feet, a thin line of glowing cyan light encircles the pipe surface. Allison thinks it's the magic responsible for the 'pumping.' This pipe is horizontal, so there shouldn't be a current in it without some kind of mechanical assistance—or in this case, magical.

After a few minutes, light appears in the distance where the pipe ends at an opening.

We emerge in a rectangular cistern in the castle's 'basement.' The top is uncovered like a swimming pool, allowing us to glide up and breach the surface. I'm treading water in a reservoir basin three times the size of my living room. It doesn't look intended for bathing, being as there are no stairs or ladders out. Also, the chamber is entirely undecorated. Six one-foot-wide bronze pipes descend straight down from the ceiling into the water, drawing it upward into the castle's plumbing system.

Wow, it is so damn strange to see an almost modern concept of plumbing in such ancient times. Allison finds it fascinating, too, but also thinks we lost so much to wars and the ravages of time. For all we know, Ancient Rome might well have had similar things... only not powered by magic. They'd have used gravity or pulleys and paddles to pump the water.

It's not difficult for us to grab the edge of the pool and pull ourselves up to dry floor. Allison dries us off with magic and hands Kingsley back his thawb. A simple ladder made of steps jutting out of the wall goes up to a brown stone square in the ceiling at the far right corner. On our left, a small passageway leads deeper into the castle at the same level as this room. From it, I hear running water. Kingsley goes up the steps, braces a hand on the stone hatch at the top, and pushes.

A few seconds later, the stair he's standing on breaks under his foot. The *crack* is startlingly loud, mostly due to the total silence in here. Kingsley falls the short distance back to the floor, managing to keep his balance while landing on his feet.

He shakes his head. "There's got to be magic sealing it closed, or it weighs like 4,000 pounds."

I point to the passageway on the left. "Should we try this?"

"Kinda looks kinda like a maintenance hallway," says Allison.

"I can hear voices down it. There must be a connection into the castle somewhere," says Kingsley, scrunching his nose. "But... it's a sewer."

"Hey, I'm not saying we should go swimming in it." I approach the passage and peek in.

A stone-walled corridor runs thirty or so feet straight ahead before cornering to the right. It's got two narrow ledges on either side of a water-filled trench. Yes, it smells like human waste in here, but *appears* clean. Two small pipes at floor level pour fresh water into the trench. I'm guessing they keep the sewer system filled and moving, also explaining why this end is cleaner. The flow's going away from the drinking water.

We follow the hallway to the corner and past it into another stretch of sewer that runs about fifty feet to a second cistern. This one contains a round basin of horror at its center. Fortunately, a reasonable amount of wet-but-cleanish floor surrounds the fecal whirlpool, offering us a path to one of two branching hallways.

Thick stone pipes hang from the ceiling over the basin, but fortunately aren't releasing any awfulness at the moment. This castle must have toilets of some form, and we're looking at the very end of the pipes. Weird thing is the sewage must be draining somewhere, though I haven't any idea where.

I'm also completely uninterested in discovering where it goes.

Allison thinks the bottom of this pit might have a small magical portal where the sewage drops out. Hopefully, they put it inside a volcano.

Kingsley's eyes are watering. Mine are, too, but not as bad. Yes, vampires have a supernatural sense of smell powerful enough where I can scent-track humans… but I've got nothing on a werewolf. Even Allison with her normal human sniffer appears close to fainting.

Not wanting to be here any longer, I make a snap decision and go into the left corridor since it contains whispering voices. Unfortunately, it leads to a maze-like arrangement of passageways. I do my best to follow the voices, but there are a lot of echoes in here.

After several dead ends and backtracking, the voices lead me to a metal grating in the ceiling. I straddle the trench, which here contains only brackish water, not straight up brown sludge, and peer up at a stone ceiling. Looks plain, almost like a vault chamber. The whispers of several women echo from the room above. Sounds like they're trying to comfort another woman who sounds terrified of being killed at any minute.

The grating is mortared in place, and it's too small for a person to fit through.

Dammit. Okay, I'm done with sewers. Time to cheat.

I grasp Allison and Kingsley's hands, and

summon the single flame, concentrating on a point in space above the grating...

Chapter Seven
Illusions of Grandeur

Such a short-distance hop occurs in a split second.

Teleporting to a spot I can physically see in front of me within like a hundred yards happens so fast the dancing flame barely has a chance to appear in my mind. We drop a foot or so to the ground since we appeared in midair.

The room we find ourselves in is saturated in a dark green hue thanks to jade tiles covering the walls as well as six octagonal columns in two rows of three, down the middle of the chamber between a pair of enormous bathtubs made from marble. The ceiling is plain stone, trim on the walls inlaid with various semiprecious stones.

A gasp comes from behind us.

I turn toward the sound.

Six women sit clustered together on a slightly

raised platform at one of the room's narrow ends. Their only clothing consists of narrow loincloths and tops, metal collars with glowing markings.

One is noticeably older than the rest, probably in her late thirties. The other five all look closer to twenty, plus or minus a year or two. The eldest and the younger woman she's embracing are both blushing and appear to have been weeping recently. The other three don't seem embarrassed at all, more resigned. Clearly, they're slaves. I doubt Elizabeth would have wasted the time to acquire these women herself. Undoubtedly, they were here before her, likely forced to work as bath attendants. I mean, the only reason I can think of to keep slaves in a giant bath chamber would be that their function is to bathe the wealthy. Guess the former administration was kinda shitty, too.

Elizabeth might not be too much of a down-grade.

Predictably, they all gawk at us in total shock since we *poofed* out of thin air.

"Shh," I whisper. "Please be quiet. We are not here to harm you."

The women all stare at me. A quick peek in their minds... and they're wondering why I'm so pale. Wow, good thing they didn't see me *before* the Red Rider situation, back when I was a bloodsucker.

I continue skimming their thoughts, on guard for potential treachery. The three calm girls mostly wonder how I came out of nowhere and are mildly worried about what we're going to do to them. Since we are unfamiliar, they don't know if they should serve us in the bath, but they also don't want to raise the alarm if we're not going to harm them. They're not terribly worried if we're here to steal or do something bad to the new queen. As expected, they've been kept in this room for a while as bath attendants to the former royal family as well as important guests. The second most prominent thought in their heads is in regard to the other two slaves—the former queen, Fahma, and her daughter, Nahari.

When I peer into *their* heads, I'm surprised to see they're more embarrassed at having become slaves and not too concerned about being damn close to naked. Seriously, those loincloths are like having a scrap of toilet paper hanging from their hips and around their breasts.

"This is unexpected," I say to the queen.

"Who are you?" asks Fahma, managing to scrape together some sort of dignity in her voice. "What do you want, dead one?"

I sigh. "I'm not one of the dead ones."

"You are drained of life," says the queen.

I smile. "We're not from around here."

The four 'experienced' slaves stand and walk over to check us out. Nahari uses her hands to hide the slave collar. Her daughter does too. Disregarding the women walking around and studying me like some alien creature—which I guess I am—I approach the queen and her daughter. "We're here to stop the woman who declared herself empress."

All six of the women gasp.

"Tis unlikely," says Princess Nahari. "You will be killed like the others."

"Or not. We have a plan."

"Then pray it is a good plan."

I look at the queen. "How did you and your daughter come to be down here?"

Fahma glances down, ashamed. "After the witch murdered my husband, she kept the men as slaves for herself. My daughter and I, she put here until she figures out what to do with us. I fear she will soon kill the two of us, perhaps turning us into monsters, too."

"Hold on." Allison raises her hand, reacting to my understanding of their words. "Will you tell them not to use 'witch' like that? Elizabeth is not a witch."

"Elizabeth isn't a witch," I repeat to them. "She's a vampire."

The women shiver. Apparently, this language has a word for vampire. Not sure if I should feel comforted or worried. Checking their thoughts tells me the concept translated accurately enough. A person who's dead but not dead. Only here, they eat the flesh of their victims rather than merely drink their blood. After they're done, their appearance changes to replace the person they killed so they can drain the life force of an entire family sharing one house. So they both feast upon the flesh *and the* psychic energy of their victims.

Ack.

I really hope that's folklore and not fact here.

"Our vampires are a little different than your understanding." I explain how we came from an alternate reality, chasing Elizabeth across dimensions. "We're a little short on time, but how would you ladies like to be set free?"

A woman to my left bows her head, fear wafting off her. Even if they do manage to escape, she expects to be caught and arrested, which is punished by abandonment in the desert, tied naked to a stone column. Okay, this society has some problems. Barbaric. Then again, humans are shitty to each other in our world, too. Some of those medieval people did *horrid* things to each other... like scaphism. Ugh. Pro tip: if bored in front of a computer, don't hit the random button on Wikipedia and read about ancient torture-slash-execution methods.

"At present, we cannot go anywhere. The pain will be unbearable," says Nahari, clutching her collar. "If we leave this room, it will feel as though our skin is peeling off."

"The collars are attached to this room?" I ask.

"No. The one who owns us has given us an order not to leave," says a slip of a woman on my right. "These"—she taps her collar—"know when we disobey."

"May I?" I ask, indicating the collar.

She nods, standing there obediently, allowing me to examine the collar up close. It's a silvery metal, about a quarter-inch thick. A thin seam at the front looks like it ought to have a keyhole or some other mechanism, but doesn't. Probably magic keeping it closed. There's a hinge at the back of her neck. It's not terribly thick. I could probably snap it open, assuming nothing bad happens.

"Allie, can you tell if these things will blow up or something if I break them?"

She walks up and examines the same woman's collar. "Not really sure. This is an enchanted item. And our reality doesn't have 'enchanters.' At least, if it did, they died out when Camelot went from reality to myth. This world's rules are different than ours."

"Would Max know?"

"Maybe. But he's an alchemist. Not a magical practitioner."

"Grr." I look around at the captive women. "Do any of you know if it's bad to break these collars off you?"

They mostly shrug or give me clueless looks.

"It is not possible to break them," says a curvy woman. "You would need the crystal key."

Hmm. Let's test that theory.

I grasp the collar of the woman who let me study it, and attempt to pull the thing apart. At first, it doesn't want to give, but after I burn a little energy to make myself stronger, it snaps as easily as if I'm breaking an ordinary latch. The collar flies open, launching a tiny metal rod across the room— the latch, apparently. Normal enough, except there's no physical mechanism to operate it. Thus, the need for magic. Or the crystal key thingie.

Nahari leaps upright and grabs two fistfuls of my shirt, shaking me. "Please, take this thing off me! I cannot bear it!"

Queen Fahma stands much more gracefully. The other four gawk at me again. So weird. Breaking the collar shocks them more than teleportation. It's a mix of doing 'the thing that shall not be done' as well as my being strong enough to snap the metal.

"You say you are not one of them." Queen Fahma raises an eyebrow.

"It's a complicated story. I'm a similar sort of being, but neither dead nor evil." I snap the collar off Nahari's neck.

Kingsley snaps a collar or two off as well. Once we have the women free, Allison conjures them some temporary garments.

I offer my hand to the queen. "Please, take my hand. All of you form a circle and grab on."

They do.

I look at Kingsley and Allison. "Be right back."

They nod.

Hmm. Can't really take them to our tent. While I don't necessarily expect the queen or any of these women to betray us to Elizabeth, it's a chance not worth taking. Also, the former queen and princess would be too recognizable. Gotta keep them hidden for now.

Aha! Idea.

The place we stopped for food, where I made the rich guy give me money… I remember a stairway going up to a second floor, probably hotel rooms—or an inn. Whatever they call them here. Can't have *mo*tels without cars, right?

It's perfect.

I picture the dancing flame and concentrate on the dark top of the stairs. The fire moves toward me, even as I move toward it... until we pass through the 'eye of the needle,' so to speak. Impressively, none of the six women make a sound as our surroundings abruptly shift.

The first door on the left closest to us leads to an empty room with a single bed. Good enough for now. I usher them inside.

"I need to get back to my friends. For now, stay in here and keep out of sight. Oh, I should warn you. The clothing Allison made for you is going to disappear in about an hour."

"We know," says the short woman. "Any object the magisters create from nothing does not last forever."

"Here." I pass a handful of lahz coins to her. "People will recognize the queen and her daughter. You can go and buy real garments for everyone, as well as food. I will return as soon as I can."

Queen Fahma nods once. "It may not be worth much given the circumstances, but you have my gratitude."

Nahari comes close to crying all over me but holds herself back. She sits quietly on the edge of the bed, rubbing her bare neck as if she can't believe the collar is gone.

"If I or one of my friends don't return in a few hours, it means we've failed to get rid of your new 'empress.' You'll probably want to leave the city in that case."

"Then I shall ask Biymimat to protect you," says the queen.

Her thoughts tell me she's referring to their goddess of life/motherhood/beauty. Slightly less powerful than their god-king, but more likely to do something because I'm a woman.

Great. I'll take all the help I can get.

I teleport back to the bath chamber—and stop short staring at two more slave women, still in collars and loincloths. "Where did you two come —"

Never mind. It's Allison and Kingsley, courtesy of a cloaking spell. Allison's thoughts gave them away. The short girl raises her arm at me... and my appearance abruptly changes into that of a tall slave girl. It's completely an illusion as I don't feel any different.

"What are you doing?" I whisper.

"It's called disguising ourselves." Allison folds her arms. She's reveling in how powerful her magic is here.

Kingsley pokes himself in the chest.

"Oh, good grief. We've lost Kingsley. He's going to be staring at his boobs for hours."

"Very funny," he mutters... and pokes himself again. I note he still sounds like his old self; that is, a man with a deep voice.

Footsteps echo from outside the room's only exit. We hurry over to the dais where the women had been seated before and pretend to be ordinary servant girls.

A woman in the black-and-red armor of the palace guard walks into the bath chamber. She's paler than I am. The thin aura of shimmery white energy clinging to her skin identifies her clearly as one of the ascendant dark masters. It's brutally sunny outside at this hour, but I'm not sure it matters to them. Normal vampires, of which Elizabeth brought a few dozen, would likely still be asleep. Anyway, I'm guessing she heard Kingsley's deep voice in here and became suspicious.

The ascendant wanders around the room, examining the gratings in the floor.

Hmm, bet she's wondering if a man's down in the sewer.

I swallow some pride and pretend to be frightened, keeping my head down. Kingsley does a fairly horrible 'scared slave girl' impression. Except his attempt to look harmless is more of a 'please take two steps closer so I can rip your head off' glare.

Somehow, the ascendant doesn't notice half the bath slaves are missing. She also doesn't appear to realize the queen and her daughter are gone. Maybe her short-term memory is on par with that of a selfie-obsessed Instagrammer. She walks over to the dais, regarding us with an expression like she's eyeing high-calorie desserts her trainer told her not to touch. Can't tell completely if she's attracted to women or merely hungry for blood, but good chance it's a bit of both.

I shift to hide my face.

The ascendant bends forward and grabs my chin, forcing me to look up at her. She licks her lips while staring at my fake chest under the simple strap. Her eyes narrow. Uh oh. She's trying to look at my thoughts, I bet. Game's up.

I summon as much energy as possible into speed, draw the Devil Killer from its dimensional sheath, and ram it into her heart. She gets her sword halfway out of its scabbard before the cross-guard of mine hits her chestplate. Fiery embers spray out of the wound, front and back, skittering over the stone floor.

Kingsley jumps on her, clamping a hand over her mouth to muffle the horrible wail of agony she gives off during the six seconds it takes for her body to blacken into a charcoal sculpture. Her tunic catches fire, the leather armor also smoldering in spots. As she begins to break apart into dusty chunks, I pull the blade out of her. Glowing, wispy strands of soul energy siphon into the blade, brightening it from jet black to glowing forge-orange.

"Ugh." Kingsley snorts a few times, backing up. "Damn that stinks."

"Whoa…" Allison stares at the light streamers going into my sword, her expression appropriate for a little kid meeting Santa Claus in person. "Epic… You destroyed her entirely."

"Yeah." I hold the sword out at arms' length. "Nice quick thinking there, big guy."

He shakes his hand off to the side. "She bit me. Damn, I hate vampire fangs. That's gonna sting for days."

I return the sword to its interdimensional pouch. "I think we should ditch the illusions, Allie."

She blinks at me, confused. "But they'll recognize us right away."

"If we look like slaves, they'll attack us, too," whispers Kingsley. "These women aren't supposed to leave this room. They see us walking around the castle in these outfits, they'll know something's wrong."

"Oh. Duh." Allison biffs herself in the forehead. She thinks for a brief moment, then weaves another spell.

Our skimpy clothes change to red-and-black armor over skirted red tunics and tall boots—just like the palace guard. Kingsley appears once again like himself, as does Allison. I assume I do too. I notice Allie has given us all healthy tans to blend in better. Smart choice.

"Much better." Kingsley rolls his head, then picks up the ascendant's discarded sword.

Chapter Eight
The Perfect Moment

Dressed like palace guards, we exit the royal bath and set about exploring the castle interior.

It feels like more of a fortress than a palace, mostly because it's a huge freakin' pyramid of solid stone. Only the outermost rooms have actual windows. The majority of hallways and chambers are windowless, lit by magical orbs roughly the size of basketballs that emit a pale yellowish-white glow.

Allison thinks it feels like we've walked onto the movie set for *Dune*. When I think 'haven't seen it,' she gawks at me, then proceeds to ramble on and on about how this castle is 'totally like the palace in the movie.' It's the aesthetic of things vaguely familiar and modern but simultaneously alien and archaic—like bronze desk lamps using magical glow balls instead of electric lights.

Being dressed like a guard offers both an advantage and a disadvantage. On the positive side, Allison's 'don't notice us' spell is still working in here. Guaranteed if we walked around in ordinary clothes, we'd probably be seen through the spell. The soldier armor illusion makes us appear plausible enough to 'belong' here.

The downside of dressing like a guard is, if we *do* get noticed, we're probably going to get caught. Not once have we seen guards moving in a group of three. They've all been alone. So, if Allison's spell fails and someone spots us, they'll instantly question what we're doing. Maybe they'll think we're on a mission?

Meanwhile, the ground floor is pretty damn big. Kitchen, dining halls, servants quarters, giant throne room—empty, armory and soldier's quarters (which we avoid like the plague), and like two dozen male slaves running around cleaning, dusting, or being domestic. They have the demeanor of employees, more like staff at a hotel than slaves. The collars, alas, are a pretty obvious marker of status. None are worried about imminent death like Fahma or Nahari, though I'm sure it's due mostly to ignorance. To Elizabeth, these guys would be walking juice boxes. She wouldn't kill them out of cruelty or for amusement as she would with the former royals, but simply because a sudden urge hit her. Or she got hungry. Or they happened to be near her when something pissed her off.

We eventually locate stairs up to the second

floor. As expected for a pyramid, the second floor is smaller than the first. It only takes us about forty minutes to recon the entire level and determine Elizabeth is not here. So, up we go again. The third floor is mostly guest bedrooms. There is, however, a library, another, much smaller, bath chamber— sans slaves—and several atriums on the outside edge with windows. No sign of a royal bedchamber anywhere yet, so it must be up more. Up one more floor.

May the fourth be with us, thinks Allison.

I groan mentally.

As soon as we step out of the switchback stairs —nice, polished obsidian by the way—two things happen simultaneously to put me on edge. Tammy grunts in my mind like she's lifting something heavy about the same time Elizabeth's voice floats down the hall. Doesn't take a genius to figure out my daughter is straining to keep us hidden.

Cautiously, I head toward the voice.

Even with Tammy guarding us, if Elizabeth makes eye contact with me, or any of us really, we're busted. Proceed directly to war, do not collect $200. A short distance from the stairwell, I pause near a set of ornate double doors on my left. They're partially open. I lean toward the gap between them for a quick peek into the room. Sure enough, Elizabeth is inside, standing by a big table with a bunch of ascendant dark masters. Looks like she's having a 'war room' meeting.

I lean back before anyone notices me. We go

past the war room to the next doorway on the opposite side. Since it's a small sitting room containing nothing more interesting than a few padded chairs and a tiny table, it seems like a safe, uninteresting, hiding spot. I dart in. Kingsley and Allison follow, and I push the door closed after they're in.

We stand in the middle of the room, Kingsley and I trying to listen in on what Elizabeth is talking about. Annoyingly, the footfalls of someone walking out in the hallway drowns her out. I hold my breath, waiting for them to go by. As they draw near, Kingsley tenses. Allison can't seem to figure out what to do with her hands.

The door swings open.

An ascendant dark master, in palace guard armor, steps into the room, giving us a quizzical look. "What the devil are you three doing in here?"

Chapter Nine
An Unexpected Visitor

For Anthony, having a completely silent head again feels alien and weird.

Now, as he waits in the tent for his mother and the others to return from their mission, he finds himself thinking of his dad.

No surprise there. His dad had, after all, been a major part of his life these past few years. And now... nothing. A void where his father had been.

A damn painful void.

Anthony kinda remembered his father being frequently busy with work, not having as much time to do fun stuff with his kids as he would've preferred. At least Dad *did* make an effort. Not like he came up with lame excuses to blow he and Tammy off. His father really had a lot of work to do running his own law practice. Later, when he got kinda nuts, he threw tons of time at the weird stuff in hopes of 'saving' Mom.

He couldn't justify the way his father had gone to war with Mom, using him and Tammy as leverage to hurt and control her. Despite it, Dad apologized to him for being like that, blaming a 'slightly-more-than-temporary psychotic break.' He knew his dad loved Mom a crap ton, and it broke him to think Mom died. For whatever reason, his father could never accept his mother hadn't been replaced by an evil clone.

Dad didn't truly understand until it had become too late.

More than any other event in Anthony's life, his father's death hurt. Having Dad's ghost haunt his brain made up for lost time, always there, always willing to listen or talk. Pops had been weird for the past few months, an edge to his mental voice like he suspected Anthony had grown tired of him and wanted him gone. Completely not true. He couldn't understand what made Dad feel like he had to go away.

Having a silent head sucked.

It reminds him his father has gone away for good.

Meanwhile, Dillon Hewitt, the big Light Warrior he finds himself hanging out with, seems to be a cool guy. Not quite as old as Dad, but he gives off a paternal or maybe 'big brother' vibe. Anthony hasn't asked the man his age, but guesses it's in the mid-thirties. He originally came from Philadelphia, but moved to Cali after Max found him as a teen.

Dillon grew up around gangs, but hadn't joined them... though he still exuded that tough 'street' vibe. Somehow, Max had a way to sense people who possessed gifts that made them good candidates for his Light Warrior School.

They all seem to know Anthony, most likely because Max knew Mom and talked about her son all the time. Almost as strange as not having his father's voice in his head anymore was the way these Light Warriors treated him. Even though he still has a few weeks to go before his sixteenth birthday, they talk *to* him, not *at* him. They seem to respect him like an equal or even a veteran of their secret brotherhood. Or maybe it's that they respect the Fire Warrior, and are only tolerating him. No, that doesn't seem right. They all seem to genuinely like *him*. The more he thinks about it, the more he feels welcome among them as an equal.

Some, like Dillon, can't do magic the same way Allison and the mystics can. When in the presence of supernatural creatures like vampires, they instead use 'magic-like' abilities to make themselves stronger and faster, enough to keep up in a fight. Others like Yasmeen, Olivia, and Madelyn reminded him of the wizards and warlocks in *World of Warcraft*. Especially so in this alternate world. They could legit cast actual spells. Of course, he'd seen Allison throwing magic bolts before, too. However, everything in this world took supernatural stuff to the next level.

He didn't have magic, at least not in the same

way they did. Anthony was strong and fast all the time. Not 'flip a car strong' like Kingsley, but Anthony had already gone somewhat past several Olympic records in terms of lifting. Definitely super human. He felt like a superhero, which was *awesome*. The best part—he could really help people.

The Light Warriors tended to help those in need whenever they could, which also sounded amazing. Talking to Dillon and Max after Mom, Kingsley, and Allison left, got him seriously considering asking if Mom would let him transfer schools. He wanted to go to the Light Warrior School. Did it really matter if he didn't technically get a real high school diploma? Max said he'd still legally have one after finishing there, even if the classes were wildly different. Only one thing kinda sucked about the idea. He wouldn't be at the same school as Topher or Dwayne. But, it's not like he hung out with either of them all that much. Topher usually ran home to hop on the computer like he did while Dwayne had sports practice almost every day. He spent more time talking to Topher over the game's voice chat than in person.

Light Warrior School wouldn't eat his entire day. He'd still go home after. Still be able to log onto the game and hang with Topher, or even have his friends over. So, yeah, they probably wouldn't even notice him not sharing a few classes. Despite his size, few other kids at school really noticed him. He tended to keep his head down.

He wondered where the Light Warrior School

was and asked Dillon.

"In a safe place."

"How safe?"

"Center of the Earth safe."

Anthony blinked. "Say again?"

"Well, not quite in the center of the Earth, as that's actually molten lava, but in one of the Earth's inner rings. There are dozens of such levels, all with different cities, languages, species, you name it. Your sister is dating an elf, am I correct?"

"Um, kind of a secret, but yeah."

"There are no secrets with the Light Warriors, Ant."

"Okay."

"But yeah, where do you think his elf race lives? Not topside."

"Topside?"

"You know, the surface of the Earth. His species of elves live in one of the inner rings, or layers. Not like the whole layer, but they take up a big chunk of it."

"You've seen such layers?"

Dillon chuckles. "You will, too, if you join the Light Warrior School. It's in a sort of medieval level within the fifth ring."

"My head is spinning."

"You'll learn all about the Inner Earth worlds. Most are filled with what people would call magical beings. Others are filled with humans, many of whom are a bit archaic."

"Like the level the Light Warriors School is

on?"

"Right. That's a straight up medieval level. Other regions are actually highly advanced. Kind of like the surface here, where some countries are more technological than others."

"How... how big are these levels?"

"In a physical sense, each would have to be smaller than the Earth itself, right? They shrink exponentially the closer one gets to the center. Some levels have single species living in them, like the elves. Others are a mixture of the magical and mundane. Populations in them aren't like on the surface. Think of them as small countries or kingdoms."

"They have air to breathe? Water? What about light?"

"You'll learn all about that at Light Warrior School, but yeah, there are massive lakes and the uppermost levels—that is, those closest to the surface—have their own oceans with large sailing vessels. The lower you go, the smaller the water sources become."

"But how does one get to these levels?"

"Oh, there are tunnels everywhere, connecting them to each other."

"Even on the surface?"

"Especially on the surface. One just needs to know where to look. There are portals into and out of the school, closely guarded, of course."

"Wow, okay. And the Light Warrior School is in such a level? Sorry, my brain is just mush."

Dillon laughs. "Yup, it's in the fifth one down. Oh, you will love Light Warriors School, Ant. The grounds around it are beautiful, magical, mist-filled, with mountains and villages and horses and a source of light that shines high in the sky."

"Does it ever get dark there?"

"Of course. The light moves through the sky, to illuminate distant lands in the fifth realm."

"And each realm has its own light source?"

"They do."

"Is it the same light source?"

"It is not, as far as I know."

"What powers the light source? Obviously, it's not the sun."

Dillon drops a heavy hand on his shoulder. "I can only tell you that magic is involved. Very powerful magic. Head spinning yet?"

"Oh yeah."

Dillon laughs and moves away to some of the other Light Warriors who are deep in some conversation.

Anthony continues standing protectively over Tammy while his sister concentrates, but wow... his mind is seriously blown. So much for having time with his friends! If things worked out, he might be living in the... center of the Earth?

He shakes his head and watches Max and some other Light Warriors study a map with the local spy, Mardet, looking for an ideal place to make the dimensional gateway. Max has about forty or fifty more Light Warriors from Europe gathering to come across and reinforce them. He took a big gamble bringing almost three-quarters of all the Light Warriors on Earth to this world... but a chance like this to finally confront Elizabeth offers too much of an opportunity to miss.

Max says something weird about thinking Elizabeth has made a big error. Like 'she'd never been this vulnerable before.' Anthony doesn't understand why, but has a hunch Max is right. He also has the weirdest feeling his Mom will need him. It doesn't leap to the level of outright worry, more a constant low-grade concern at the back of his mind.

"Anthony?" asks a deep voice, slightly behind him on the right. "Might I have a word with you?"

He twists to look.

A blond figure stands partially in the tent's only entrance, tall, broad shouldered and like something out of one of those boring old paintings by Raphael or DaVinci or something. His tunic and cloak appear similar to the style of everyone else, though a mirror-shiny silver breastplate stands out as strange. The man is of indefinable age, simultaneously youthful and wizened, possessing the physique of a warrior, and had the spark of a scholar in his expression.

Anthony's first thought is 'they hired a blond guy to play Superman.' As the initial shock of seeing a figure so out of place for this environment waned, a sense of reverence and authority comes over Anthony. Within seconds of being in the man's presence, he somehow feels as if he's looking at a teacher he knows well and respects.

"Um, sure."

The man steps back and holds the tent flap open. Anthony starts after him, pausing momentarily when he realizes no one else in the tent notices him, or seems concerned that a stranger has arrived. Anthony shrugs and exits the tent. He senses an odd sort of peace emanate from the man. Anthony looks around. People go about their day, seeming oblivious to the two of them standing there. Weirdly, Anthony feels invisible at the moment.

"You are wondering who I am?"

"You could say that."

The handsome man smiles just as a great pair of feathered wings stretch out from behind his back, similar in appearance to Mom's, only bright silvery-white. Unlike Mom's this man's wings gave off a continuous radiance. "I am the Archangel Michael."

Chapter Ten
Angelic

Upon hearing the words, Anthony knows them as truth.

He stands a little straighter. "I'm Anthony Moon."

The angel smiles, retracts his wings. "It is good to finally meet you, young warrior."

"Are you here because of Elizabeth?"

"I am not. I am here because it is time to make you aware of your destiny."

"My destiny?"

"Walk with me, young warrior."

"But my sister..."

"Is being watched over by one of my own. She is in good hands. The best."

Anthony looks back at the tent, through a crack in the flap, and sees a golden glow emanate from within. Anthony knows his mother is sort of an agent for the Archangel Azrael, also known as the Angel of Death. So, yeah, he's been hearing about 'archangels' for some time now. He also knows Michael also trained his mother in the use of the Devil Killer, albeit briefly. Not quite like the training she's been receiving lately from that old vampire in the Hollywood Hills.

Together, the archangel and Anthony move through tents. No one seems to notice them, especially not the pretty girl about Anthony's age. He averts his eyes, refusing to be distracted. Anthony knows he's always had strong willpower, one that only seems to be getting stronger.

"I'm here to say you've been chosen to join our ranks."

Anthony stares at the tall man—angel—his brain struggling to process what he'd just heard. "You mean after I die?"

"No." Michael turns and smiles. "Your mortal death has already come and gone, young warrior. For now, you need not suffer the burden again. When the time is right, you will know. Your task at present is to learn, and to assist those in need of your aid."

"Learn? I was just told of the Light Warrior School."

"A good place of learning, surely."

"Why are you telling me this now?"

"Now is a pivotal time for you, young one." Michael clasps his hands behind his back as they weave through the tent village; a weird-looking hairy dog is the only creature seemingly aware of their presence. "You see, the nature of your father's soul, while it remained stored within your body, corrupted the whole of your being, holding you back from the path set before you."

Anthony wants to feel upset at this angel for telling him his father was a 'corruption,' but can't. He recognized the truth of it months ago, despite not understanding what he knew or why. That truth manifested as an indefinable sense of something being 'not right,' the ickiness whenever his father projected out of his body or manifested some effect in the real world. Dad said he felt as though Anthony wanted him to go away. Perhaps at a subconscious level, Anthony's psyche considered Dad an unwelcome dark energy, opposite to his nature.

Michael nods. "Yes. Part of you knew. Part of you did not want to know."

"Is Dad going to be happy where he is now?" asks Anthony, surprising himself at his voice not faltering from sorrow.

"For a time, he will be quite happy. Eventually, as those versions of your mother and sister age, challenges will arise. Many years from now, the version that remains an eternal child of the night will be taken in by a group of vampires."

"Like a little kid at a hippie commune, where everyone's basically his parent." Anthony blinks. "How did I know that?"

Michael pats him on the shoulder. "We know

certain things when we need to know them, young one. In this case, being aware of your child self's future, knowing he is safe—even if in a different world—must have been important for you to know."

In a way, it had been. Now, he no longer worried about Dad, or little Anthony.

Thinking about becoming an angel both excited and scared him. Angels didn't hang around on Earth. His mom mentioned they lived in the sun. She learned this from her own guardian angel, Ishmael, who sort of had the hots for her—so much so that he'd allowed the attack that made her a vampire, doing nothing to step in to stop it.

"Think of the sun as our home base," says the archangel, clearly reading his thoughts. "A fitting home for the Fire Warrior, eh?"

"Wait... is the Fire Warrior..."

"Yes, Anthony. It is a form of warrior angel. The strongest among us."

"Whoa."

"Whoa indeed. And yes, some of us have been angels from the beginning. Others are promoted to our ranks. You would be one of them... if you agree. An angel apprentice, if you will. However, you need not make the decision now."

To Anthony, being a guardian angel came sort of... naturally to him. He always wanted to protect the innocent, to help those in need. But...

"You are nervous because you do not wish to leave your mother and sister."

"Yeah."

"Your future is already set in motion, if you choose to accept it. Ours is a free will universe. However, you do not need to make a decision or to leave them yet. Or even soon. All things in life are gradual. Your father's last request of you was to defend your sister. I see no reason why you would need to break your promise. Now or ever."

Anthony slouches in relief. "Okay. Helping people is cool. I'm definitely into that. And being an angel sounds awesome. I don't even have to think about it. It's a freakin' yes."

Michael smiles. "I suspected as much."

"Oh, wait… do the Light Warriors know I'm like an apprentice angel now?"

"They've been sensing it, yes."

"No wonder they've been acting odd around me."

"Indeed."

"Umm. The Fire Warrior didn't come from the elemental plane of fire, did he?"

Michael shook his head. "No. He and you are the same. You might say he is your future state pulled back through time to aid you now."

"So I'm going to be stuck like that permanently some day?"

"Stuck is not the right word." Michael's appearance changes to that of an old man. Seconds later, he becomes a nine-year-old boy. Then, he changes into Mr. Hoff, one of the janitors at Anthony's school. "We can appear to humans however we desire. The form you assume at any moment does not define your true nature, only the way in which the world perceives you." Michael changes into a floor lamp, hopping along the sandy earth.

Anthony chuckles. "Can I do this?"

The lamp shapeshifts back into Michael's original appearance. "In time."

"Cool."

Michael holds an arm out, palm up. A small flame appears in his hand, rapidly growing to the size of a tennis ball before stretching taller. Anthony stares in awe at a silvery broadsword levitating out from the archangel's hand like a rabbit coming out of a magician's hat. The handle and cross-guard are gold, and relatively plain in design. Fire coats the entire blade, rippling in the breeze like an Olympic torch. He expects more heat to waft from it than does.

"That's for me, isn't it?"

"It is."

"May I?" asks Anthony.

"Of course."

Anthony gingerly takes hold of the blade. The instant his skin made contact with the grip, a shock races up his arm, tingling in his fingers as well as his heart. He gasps, caught off guard by the near-painful sensation. Confusion as to why the sword zapped him lasts only a second or two. This blade touched his soul. No one can steal it from him. Until or unless he willingly gives it away, the sword would appear whenever he calls it.

He holds it up, gazing into the flames peeling from the mirror-finished blade.

It tells him it will burn demons, dark masters, undead, and any creature made from energy in opposition to the angels. Despite being a solid sword wreathed in fire, it can't inflict the smallest scratch on an innocent mortal, only one with a soul as black as a demon's.

"Wow. I umm…" Anthony keeps staring at the sword. The part of him which remained a fifteen-year-old is thrilled at getting such an awesome sword, but he keeps his emotions in check. He's been getting better and better at doing just that. "I don't really know what to say. But thank you."

"It is less of a gift and more merely receiving the tools you will need to fulfill your task."

"I understand." Anthony lowers the sword. As soon as he thinks to 'put it away,' the blade disappears. Anthony knows it's available to him whenever he needs it. He needs only to think of it. "So, that's it? I'm an angel apprentice now?"

"You are what you have already been for the last, nearly nine years, young warrior. Consider this a probationary period." Michael winks—and vanishes.

"Whoa," whispers Anthony.

Certain things make sudden sense: how the idea of traipsing across dimensions never frightened him. Why he didn't fear Elizabeth as much as concern about what she might do to his sister or mother. Also, why he felt the need to be here, and to a lesser extent, with the Light Warriors. He suspects the archangels want him to become their 'man on Earth' so to speak. Like a CIA agent stationed permanently in East Berlin during the Cold War, he'd be here, hopefully until his sister no longer needs him.

As far as I'm concerned, she's going to need my protection until she goes back around for another spin.

The idea of watching Tammy turn into an old lady and die scares him more than facing Elizabeth. But he shouldn't fear it. Her soul will circle around into another lifetime. The qualities responsible for making Tammy would still be at the core of her being. Perhaps in the next life, she'd enjoy things she missed out on in this one, like a normal family and a life free of bizarre, terrifying experiences and supernatural powers.

He has a feeling whoever she became in her next life might still have some telepathy, though.

Time to head back to Tammy, and his post.

Chapter Eleven
A Bushel of Dark Masters

It's been a really long time since someone barged into a room and caught me doing something I shouldn't be doing.

No, I never had an embarrassing moment at home as a teen where someone walked in on me 'taking matters into my own hands' so to speak. In a house with three brothers, a sister I shared a bedroom with, and parents... just no. Way too much chaos for me to even attempt finding privacy. My brothers, on the other hand, used to take suspiciously long in the bathroom sometimes.

Last time I had the gasp plus 'oh shit' reaction to someone barging into a room happened in college. I'm a little fuzzy on the details. Linda—my dorm mate—either caught me with this guy Gabe I dated for like four months, or walked in on me smoking weed. Yes, I'd been a bit of a wild child back in the day.

Anyway, in this case, the thing I'm not supposed to be doing isn't embarrassing at all. It's sneaking into an enemy castle. Allison's provided an illusion spell to disguise our clothing by making it look like palace guard armor. She's also given us one hell of a fake suntan, so to speak.

The ascendant dark master who just walked into the sitting room where we decided to hide is making a face at me kinda the way Marcellus Wallace looked at Butch in the movie *Pulp Fiction* when he saw him sitting in his car. Yeah, that's definitely a 'what the hell are *you* doing here' stare, mixed with a tiny bit of 'uh oh.'

Time seems to slow to a crawl as I speed myself up.

I reach for the Devil Killer. The ascendant hasn't quite decided if they want to commit to attacking me or run for help before Kingsley launches himself at the guy. The guard pivots, arms out wide as though he intends to catch and Judo flip the big guy to the floor. The ascendant is not, however, expecting Kingsley to shapeshift into a tiger-sized wolf in midair. While the dark master *does* succeed in grabbing the big furry beast around the body, it doesn't stop the enormous, fanged mouth.

Kingsley practically inhales the vampire's entire head, wrenching the ascendant into the room out of sight from the hallway. He chomps down, throwing a spray of exceptionally dark blood everywhere. I stare in momentary horror at the decapitated body lying on its front side, the bite so deep it scooped out a little torso as well as the entire neck. Allison finally reacts to Kingsley's leap. She raises her arms in preparation to cast a spell. Seeing as how the ascendant is *very* unconscious, I relax my supernatural speed and the world returns to normal time.

Allison relaxes, too, and clamps her hands over her mouth to stifle the disgusted noises she can't help but make at the gore. Blood seeps out of the hole where the neck used to be. No arterial spurting due to undeath. Kingsley stumbles to the side, retches once, then spits out the severed head/neck. He convulses three more times with increasing violence before barfing. Watching a dog throwing up is kinda nauseating. Watching a 700-pound wolf hork up chunks of person is an order of magnitude worse. However, I used to have two toddlers. The geyser of chunder and gagging sounds don't upset my stomach, though I do grimace.

Allison, unfortunately, has never raised kids.

She turns green, looks away, and also throws up.

After twenty seconds and Kingsley showing no sign of slowing down—seriously, he's embarked on an epic barf-a-thon like something hit him with a magical vomiting curse—I run over and start patting him on the back.

"What's wrong?"

Kingsley, for obvious reasons, doesn't reply. He keeps on gagging and retching, throwing up blasts of partially digested food and orangey-brown slime while twitching and shaking as if every flea in this universe teleported into his fur all at once.

"Is he okay?" rasps Allison.

"Not sure… he doesn't like fresh meat. Never realized it hits him this hard."

In between projectile streams of nasty coming out of his mouth, the big guy growls angrily. By some absolute miracle, no one in the castle hears this. At least, if they do, they haven't come running to check.

Kingsley convulses again, releasing a blast of black vapor. The inky smoke wisps out of his mouth into a tendril of shadow, flowing into the ascendant's remains. The corpse's neck begins to regrow fast enough to observe regenerating, like watching time lapse video of a snowman melting in reverse. It's fascinating and disgusting in equal measure. Much the same way some people have an instinctual 'kill it with fire' reaction to the sight of large, hairy spiders, I promptly stab the Devil Killer into the ascendant's torso.

The blade emits a squelching noise as if I've touched searing hot steel to flesh. His head ceases regenerating about a third of the way done, not much above the jaw. Allison grimaces at the gory sight, but doesn't suffer long. The body abruptly turns into a charcoal mannequin before disintegrating, leaving a pile of inky dust and smoldering armor. Glowing strands of spirit energy well up from the mess, drawn into the Devil Killer, which vibrates and shakes in my grip. I grab it in both hands, fighting the violent forces trying to knock it out of my grasp. The blade heats up to glowing from the energy released by the dark master's soul... or whatever it is they have.

Allison thinking I look like one of the *Ghostbusters* strikes me so randomly off guard I damn near cackle.

As soon as the stream of spectral energy is gone, I wave my sword around to cool it off.

"Ugh," mutters Kingsley, now back in his human form.

"Are you okay?" I peer back at him.

He's sprawled on the floor, curled in a ball and holding his stomach. Despite his physical clothes having been shredded by his rapid transformation, the illusion of armor is still on him, so he appears dressed.

"I haven't gone through anything like that since 1969." He sits back on his heels. "Note to self: do *not* eat these guys. That dark master started fighting with mine for control of *me*. Was close there for a few moments."

"Is this where I'm supposed to say the stupid, pointless thing?" I ask.

He glances sideways at me. "Which pointless thing is that?"

"Dark masters aren't supposed to be able to possess other immortals." I keep waving the sword. It's no longer glowing, but still hot enough to cauterize a wound.

Kingsley nods. "Aye. Shouldn't happen, but it almost did."

"Which is why it's kinda pointless to say it shouldn't be possible." I put the Devil Killer away, it can cool off in its sheath for a bit.

"Two things out of the norm are at work here." Allison holds up a finger. "One, entirely different world. Two, ascendant masters are new. Thus, new rules."

"Don't forget there is no Void here." Kingsley stands, hand pressed to his stomach. "I sincerely doubt I'm going to be anything close to hungry for a while."

I pat him on the back. "Sure. As soon as you smell meat, you're going to forget all about this."

"What happened in 1969?" asks Allison.

"Woodstock." He smiles. "Far, far too much booze… and other things."

"A werewolf on quaaludes can't be a pretty sight," I deadpan.

"Anyway," says Kingsley. "Eating these guys is a bad idea."

I cringe at the pile of black dust. "Wasn't planning on it."

Chapter Twelve
Best Laid Plans

For most of my life, I didn't believe in anything supernatural.

Sure, I spent a couple years as a kid wondering if faeries might have existed, but Mary Lou's reaction to my childish awe over seeing one had been fairly crushing. Guess you could say I'd had a certain sense of pride about me, even as a kid. It bothered me to have my older sister laugh at me and tell me to stop acting like a *little* kid.

She kinda wounded my sense of wonder, and my parents finished it off. Nine-year-olds who understand the idea of starving to death tend to develop a bit of a grim outlook. For normal kids, food is something the parents make magically appear at meal times. I knew exactly where it came from—and how we didn't have a lot of it—way too young. Reality checks suck, especially when the bank is constantly overdrawn.

As a result, I didn't trust anything not right in front of my eyes. This included religion. Granted, I didn't hate it, merely thought it something of a story grown-ups told themselves to feel better about stuff they couldn't control. However, feeling the Origin's presence when Jeffcock—my sire—went back to it has made me rethink stuff.

Hiding in this sitting room while we killed an ascendant dark master and Kingsley barfed his brains out—not a quiet process by any means, mind you—and *not* being discovered also makes me more amenable to the idea of *something* being out there to watch my back. Maybe Ishmael's skulking around trying to make up for slacking off and letting me be ambushed by the vampire. Maybe Max and his Light Warrior mystics have blanketed me in 'luck spells' or something.

Who knows?

Point being—we made a bunch of noise in here and aren't up to our eyeballs in badness.

Allison and I creep up to the door, listening against it like a pair of tweens eavesdropping on an older sister's phone call with their boyfriend. Kingsley goes back to wolf form so his ears are bigger and better.

Elizabeth and multiple other voices, both male and female, are in the midst of discussing how to proceed. It's getting kind of heated in there, which might explain how none of them heard us. The most sensitive microphone in the world wouldn't pick up a conversation in another room down the hall if it's placed next to a shouting match.

Seems as though Elizabeth wants to take the three nearest cities over right away, using the forces at her disposal, while the others are all proposing slightly different ways of building up strength here first. I'm astonished to hear her giving a shit what someone else thinks at all. She never struck me as the sort of leader who cared about anyone's opinion other than her own. But I suppose even Julius Caesar had advisors. There has to be some reason Elizabeth is open to suggestions now.

Crazy to think how often I shut her down in my own mind. I regularly sealed her tight in various mental prisons... only to see her leak back out. After all, mental prisons need attention, and I had a life to live. As soon as I took my focus away, the prison began to weaken.

And now, here she was... commanding armies and planning to take over an entire world. I had simply been one step of many. Likely I was just a distant, possibly unpleasant memory.

Time to give her a reminder...

A somewhat effeminate man says, "If we present ourselves as too great a threat before we have the strength to resist a committed invasion, we are only inviting them to wipe us out. Once we seize the cities surrounding Iskariya, the neighboring kingdoms will see us as a threat to put down before we become unstoppable."

"Pierre is right," replies a man with a voice so deep he could probably sing for a Johnny Cash cover band. "We have the opportunity now to grow our power in the dark, so to speak. We should do so. When the remaining nations of this world realize you are far more than a simple change of monarchy, it will be too late for them to stop you."

Elizabeth grumbles.

"It would be wise not to be impatient," says a sultry woman. "Dormund and Pierre speak with sound reasoning. We still have a 167 unbound masters waiting in line to merge with hosts. The castle is a veritable haunted house."

Six people chuckle.

"What shall we do about them, Amina?" asks Elizabeth.

"Well," replies the woman. "Each of the three options before us presents various advantages and drawbacks. If you are in a hurry, bringing them forward as... what is it you are calling them now? Ascendant?"

"Where did you get that from?" Pierre chuckles. "Sounds a bit lofty, like we've achieved Zen."

"I rather like it," says Dormund. "It conveys a sense of power."

"Exactly why I called them that," replies Elizabeth in a superior tone.

Lying bitch. She knows damn well she got the word out of my brain because I needed a way to differentiate them from ordinary vampires.

"Yes, well, the process of gathering the power

necessary to emerge as an ascendant takes weeks in this dimension." Amina sighs. "We should have stayed where we were and made our move after we all ascended."

Dormund emits a displeased grunt. "And gamble all of our number being wiped out? We must establish a sanctuary. Those who remain unbound do not accept the risk."

"You overstate things, my friend," replies another man.

"Immaterial." Elizabeth pauses, probably tapping her foot. "In the third dimension, the process by which we ascend takes too long for our needs."

"Only due to your impatience," says Amina. "You asked us to speak as a council of equals. For what reason do you feel this need to rush and be haphazard?"

Wow, she's brave.

I can practically feel Elizabeth's anger from here. She does not like sharing power. The other dark masters would be fools to expect any sort of empress-advisor relationship will last very long once she obtains greater power. She must be nervous things will go wrong here before she can reach a state similar to a demigod.

"We have come too far and are too close to fail," says Elizabeth.

"I agree!" yells Amina. "Exactly why it is best to be methodical. Ascending takes too long and many of those who wait will not take the step until the sanctuary exists. Our choices are between vampires or exalted."

"The exalted are not hindered by sunlight," says Dormund. "They would be the fastest means to achieve an army superior to mortals."

"Exalted are not immortal," says Pierre.

"Your point?" asks Dormund. "If their human dies, they merely take another one. Possession is a few hours at most and requires no more than a pliable mind."

"Vampires, though they are hampered by sunlight, have advantages." Pierre exhales hard. "The exalted are a little stronger and faster than mortals. Vampires become *much* more so, and have additional abilities beyond brute advantage."

Amina sighs. "Exalted achieve full strength right away. It takes a vampire almost a year to reach the same power."

"Yes, but they are *far* more difficult to kill," snaps Pierre. "No one in this world understands us, or silver."

"They have magic," says Dormund. "We have already seen in the minds of the former king's minions their 'magisters' possess the ability to incinerate us fatally."

"How many of them could there possibly be?" asks Elizabeth dismissively.

"One is too many until we have a sanctuary." Pierre huffs.

"Ascendancy offers the most power," says a different woman with a German accent. "We have no need to rush. We should work to ascend all of our number. Possessing humans, vampire or exalted, is distasteful. It's as repulsive as putting on someone else's undergarments. I detest having my power muted by the presence of a lesser being."

"Bringing everyone across as ascendants will take over three years," says Elizabeth, her tone impatient.

"The holdouts do not wish to ascend," says Dormund. "And I cannot fault them. They fear mortality."

"We are not vulnerable," says Elizabeth. "If these bodies are destroyed, our essence will return to the fifth dimension and regenerate a new form."

I grin to myself. Don't be so sure about that, Liz.

"They are not convinced of this," replies Dormund. "Without a Void, destruction in this body could be permanent. They do not wish to take the chance."

"Even if Elizabeth is right and we will return to the fifth," says Pierre, "the process takes three months. We could possess a new human host in mere hours after losing this body."

"You have found a way to rebind us?" asks Amina.

Elizabeth lets out a long sigh, like I'm reminding twelve-year-old Tammy she still needs to take the garbage outside. "Yes. However, it will involve creating another version of the Void linked to this world. A hidden sanctum not intended to trap us, but offer shelter instead. One we can freely leave at will."

"I am not convinced our souls will reach the fifth dimension if we are killed in this form," says Dormund. "We are risking everything by pouring all our power into physicality. As vampires, were-wolves, and other beings possessing mortals, the humans served as armor. Without a Void to return to, we had free rein to slip right into another human. But in this form… destruction may be final. I must agree with Lena."

"Some risk is acceptable, but we are doing too much," says the German-sounding woman… likely Lena.

Amina and Dormund murmur in agreement.

"The others fear this as well," says the unnamed man. "Dormund is right. They refused to take on a physical form already because they fear final destruction. The Origin still seeks to draw us into its grasp. Without the shield of a mortal, we are too close to final death."

Elizabeth scoffs. "Do you not relish the greater power? Everything you have ever attained, at your fingertips. Mortals are in the way. Thorsen, do you not bask in power you've not wielded since the days you walked this Earth as a mortal? It would take you hundreds of years as a vampire to even come close."

"For many, reclaiming the power we once manipulated is worth the risk." Lena lets out a long, deep breath. "For others, it is not. They will not ascend until there is a sanctuary and a means to prevent the loss of our being."

"Creating a sanctum will take time and resources," says Elizabeth. I sense her jaw clenching.

She and her advisors lapse into a heated debate about whether it is best to work on a new Void so the remaining 167 non-corporeal dark masters can ascend with peace of mind, or if they should concentrate on a more rapid army to conquer the land. If option two, do they reinforce Iskariya via the remaining dark masters possessing mortals directly as Exalted or turn them into vampires. Apparently, those superhuman-but-not-vampire guards are something Elizabeth calls 'Exalted.' Dark masters possessing still-living humans without turning them into undead.

Allison thinks they sound as indecisive and superstitious as the people who call in to her radio show. She's right. They totally do. Especially Elizabeth. She reminds me of a modern version of Cleopatra who's trying to remodel the palace in the middle of a war and everything's going mildly wrong at once. Not disastrously wrong, more like the delivery guy showed up with coral-colored curtains instead of aqua.

She's sorta the bridezilla of the apocalypse.

Wouldn't want to be the DJ at her wedding, thinks Allison.

Stop, you're going to make me laugh.

They'll never hear us. Feels like we're backstage at an episode of Dance Moms.

Nah. Those moms are more violent.

Elizabeth, who thus far has been all about expanding as fast as possible, finally shouts for everyone to be quiet.

Silence hangs over the castle—or at least this hallway—for a moment.

"You do all appreciate the need to increase our power to the point where nothing in this world can threaten it, correct?" asks Elizabeth.

The others murmur agreement.

"Though I want to expand our territory, we shall focus on establishing a dark sanctum first. Pierre has convinced me. We must safeguard our own existence as a first step before too many in this world become aware of our true power."

Pierre emits a happy noise. The others also sound content, though a bit surprised.

Honestly, I am, too. Elizabeth deferring to others' suggestions, especially when they're contradicting her wants, is super rare. The fact that ascendant dark masters are vulnerable to complete death would explain why they had so little interest in fighting me back in Venezuela. Granted, I *am* carrying a sword capable of killing anything, so their avoiding *me* doesn't necessarily prove anything. Not sure they understand how wicked my sword is, though Elizabeth does. She was with me first hand as I took on the devil himself.

Could ascendant dark masters be killed by something other than my sword?

Sure, some of the Light Warriors hit them with silver bolts, but I can't remember watching any ascendant masters die. All the crossbow strikes I saw had been in non-vital areas. Bear in mind, this is like wondering who exactly punched who in the face during a fight at a soccer stadium. The war around the portal in Venezuela had been super chaotic. For all I know, a handful of ascendants exploded into ash.

Question is, if an ascendant dark master is destroyed by something other than my sword, would they go to the fifth dimension like Elizabeth thinks they will, or do they go flying up to the Origin like the others are afraid? When I barfed Elizabeth out way up in the higher dimensions, she essentially became the first ascendant dark master— a vampire residing in a body they generated from magical energy. It's as close as they can ever come to being their former selves again.

I'm nowhere near enough of a witch, alchemist, or magic-user to understand the process by which they create these bodies. But, I imagine with great power comes great instability. But… when I destroyed those guards, my sword ate wispy bits of spirit energy after the fact, as if it sucked up their wraiths after the body disintegrated. To me, it says merely destroying an ascendant dark master *won't* permanently destroy them. My sword is, as they say, the bee's knees. However, I'm not going to tell them that.

What difference does it make? asks Allison. *Even if killing them here sends them back to the fifth floor, they'll be out of commission for three months like the one guy said.*

Yeah, but if anything else but the Devil Killer takes Elizabeth out, she'll return.

Allison gives me an 'oh, yeah. Good point' look.

"Lena, Thorsen, gather the *seven* and see they have everything they need for the creation of a new dark sanctum," says Elizabeth. "Once it exists, we shall ascend all our numbers. For now, the shadows should all claim humans, preferably those with bodies accustomed to warfare, making more exalted to defend the city while we work to build the sanctum. Doing so will not bind them to the human so deeply as vampirism. The link is as impermanent as the life of the host. Far easier to ascend them later. These Exalted will defend Iskariya from any outside threats. For now, we hold this city and will send Iliana, Grigori, and Piotr to the other three cities within this kingdom. They will remain undetected and influence the minds of the dukes to keep them loyal."

"This world is ours," says Dormund. "I like this plan."

Pierre claps. "Agreed."

The advisors leave the war room. Allison and I keep listening at the door to their soft footsteps going away in the opposite direction. Thank goodness none are coming our way. Still, almost imperceptible finger tapping within the room tells me one person stayed behind. Gotta be Elizabeth.

Holy crap, she's alone.

Allison detects me thinking about ambushing her and covers her mouth to stop from gasping.

Since there is no arguing going on, the slightest noise we make will surely reach Elizabeth's ears.

Maybe it's stupid, but this is a chance I have to take.

I ease the door to the sitting room open and peer out into the hall.

A shadow stretches out from the war room doorway. Eep! I duck back out of sight.

Elizabeth pads into the corridor. All three of us hold our breath, lest she hear it.

"Where are you?" mutters Elizabeth, almost too quiet for human ears to pick up.

Dammit!

"You're here, aren't you?" whispers Elizabeth. "Where are you…?"

Son of a bitch. I pull the Devil Killer. She's going to sense me any second.

"Where are you, little Tammy?" whispers Elizabeth. "What are you doing in my world? Oh, you aren't reaching across worlds. You're actually here."

Shit. Shit. Shit.

She hasn't heard or felt *me*.

"I feel you… out there… somewhere."

Allison rests a hand on my shoulder. She wants me to wait since we haven't been made, hoping Elizabeth will go back into the room out of sight from the corridor. Then we can strike.

"She is here," says Elizabeth in a whispery,

polyphonic voice like five of her speaking at once. *"Find her."*

This bitch just sent *something* to hunt my kid.

Never heard the multi-voice thing before, and I don't like it.

Nope. Not a bit.

She's messing with my daughter. Screw this. Tammy doesn't have much chance to defend herself against whatever Elizabeth just told to find her to begin with. If she's concentrating on shielding everyone, any chance she *does* have drops to zero. I can't ask her to keep hiding us when it's going to leave her so vulnerable.

I raise the Devil Killer and charge out into the hall.

Chapter Thirteen
Pandemonium

Elizabeth is standing by the door to the war room, facing a pair of shadow figures.

The bitch is sending disembodied dark masters after my daughter.

All three turn toward me in response to my running footsteps echoing in the stone-floored corridor. I teleport myself like twenty-five feet, appearing behind both shadows—and thrust the Devil Killer into one. Ember sparks leap from the edges of the blade as it shudders in my grip, almost as if the Origin has reached through it to grab this fiend who has eluded their fate for so long.

A sheath of glowing white energy forms around the blade. In seconds, the radiance spreads all throughout the vaguely human-shaped form before it shrinks down, absorbed into the sword.

I hide the surprise of my impulsive plan

working and stab at the second shadow figure—but it darts away out of my reach.

"Touch my daughter and you will find oblivion," I say, scowling at the zooming shadow figure.

Elizabeth shrieks angrily and swings her arm at me in the manner of a sword strike. I react on instinct despite her empty hand. Lucky for me, too, as her caustic blade appears out of nowhere an instant before our weapons cross, spraying acidic droplets and fiery sparks all over the floor.

We glare at each other for a fraction of a second before she shoves me away hard enough to throw me off my feet. I land on my back, managing to reverse somersault upright and raise my defenses before she can stab me again. Our blades cross three times in a second before she ducks my counterattack going for her face and scrambles backward out of reach.

Elizabeth grabs at the air with her left hand and swings her arm to the side.

An invisible force wraps around me, slamming me face-first into the wall on my right, crushing a small table made from woven palm leaves. I feel like a bug hitting a stone windshield, except I didn't pop open. She swings her arm the other way, and I zoom across the hall, smacking into the opposite wall.

Ouch.

Guess she's past the point of talking.

An energy bolt from Allison slams into the middle of Elizabeth's back. Tiny flames flicker within a roughly one-inch hole straight through her. Still standing by the door to the sitting room, my witchy friend stares wide-eyed at the damage her spell caused. Uh oh. We might have a hard time convincing Allison to leave this world and go home.

Elizabeth glances down at her chest and sighs with no more concern than if Allie had spilled white wine on her dress. Kingsley, back in wolf form, comes barreling down the corridor after his Lizzie chew toy.

I draw my arm back to insert the Devil Killer into the nice pre-drilled hole Allie made for me, but someone rushing me from behind makes me reflexively turn to defend. Having to force myself to lose a chance to strike Elizabeth down makes my defense sluggish. A brute of a man with long black hair grabs me by what he thinks is my armor. Seriously, this dude could be in the WWE. He'd make half of those guys look small. I get a brief look at a dark scar crossing his entire face from temple to jaw before he hauls me off my feet and throws me into the wall again.

What he thought was leather armor is really only fabric. I know he didn't mean to, but being grabbed by my boobs and thrown with forklift strength hurts more than my face hitting the wall. I bounce off the stone and crash to the floor, moment-arily stunned by pain severe enough I'm worried he tore the girls clear off my chest. He'd probably been intending to bear-hug me from behind and hold me down for Elizabeth to do whatever.

A puddle of fire appears beneath Elizabeth—has to be Allison. Dancing embers float into the air from the yawning portal. The bitch emits a yelp of surprise, but there's no fear in it. Sounds like Mary Lou when she almost steps on the stray cat who haunts her back yard. Fire scorches the side of her dress as she leaps away.

Allison screams. Growling and grunting come from behind me.

Pushing past the pain, I force myself up to all fours.

A skinny male ascendant with a big nose has Allison off her feet in a one-handed grip around her neck. He presses her against the wall and winds a narrow tapestry around her a few times, tying her arms to her sides and leaving her hanging there like a Christmas tree ornament. She looks furious, but at least the guy didn't kill her. An ascendant getting the drop on her would have been over fast if he'd wanted to take her life.

A patter of bare feet comes from my left. I spring upright, sword in a ready pose. A red-haired woman in a red dress like something straight out of Victorian London rushes at Kingsley, wielding a seven-foot-tall metal candlestick like a spear. This girl takes pale to the next level. She's like an undead version of a Disney princess… if they allowed Disney princesses to age into their late twenties.

She clobbers Kingsley over the head with the candlestick, bending it and knocking the big wolf off the brutish guy he'd been scuffling with, sending Kingsley sliding like a curling stone right at Elizabeth. The undead princess's 'oops' expression tells me she didn't intend to launch him at Lizzy.

The new empress leaps out of the way of the tumbling monster wolf, swiping her sword at him as he goes by—but fortunately misses. I lean back, ducking under a thin line of green acid flying off the tip of her sword, which hits the wall behind me, sizzling. Allison struggles at the tapestry, kicking her legs and bouncing in an effort to rip free. The redhead helps the brute up while two men in red-and-black armor rush past them at me.

I can tell in an instant they're alive, 'exalted' as Elizabeth calls it, but briefly possessed by dark masters. I can't mind control them, don't want to kill them, but have few options. The guy on the left comes in, falchion sword raised high. The other guy's angling on me for a stabbing thrust at my gut. I fling myself at the one holding his arm way up, getting under his reach while sidestepping the other man's thrust.

I body check the exalted so hard his sword pops out of his grip and he goes flying off his feet, sliding down the hall on his back. The other man misses, jabbing his sword into the wall with a metal-on-stone *clank*. I spin, slashing the Devil Killer into the back of his right knee. He screams in pain and collapses. Trying to avoid killing the guy, I kick him in the head, flinging him face-first against the wall and knocking him out cold… probably with a broken nose and jaw, to boot.

The redhead grabs the falchion from the guy who dropped it and charges me. I dodge, ducking and weaving right. She lands a grazing slash on my left arm as she passes, but spins fast enough to get her sword up to block my counterattack. Our blades ring off each other, the Devil Killer melting a deep nick in her ordinary weapon. She backpedals, gawking at the quarter-inch notch. Not sure what their falchions are made of, but it isn't steel. Even if it was, an angelic blade should easily snap mundane swords.

Kingsley the wolf flips back onto his feet and savages a nearby exalted who made the unfortunate mistake of being near him. The skinny ascendant turns at the horrific sounds, and goes after him with a sword of his own. He and the big wolf crash back and forth in the corridor, destroying palm tables and woven chairs. Amid a rip of fabric, Allison's tapestry gives out above her head and dumps her back onto her feet. She easily frees her arms now that her weight isn't holding the material tight around her.

The redhead finds a secondary burst of courage and tries to take my head off. I block easily, press the attack, and push her into a retreat over a series of strikes. She parries me each time, but is clearly straining to keep up with me, more due to technique than raw speed. We're about even in terms of reflexes, but she doesn't seem as experienced using a sword. Not that I'm even close to a master, but working with Sebastian helped a lot in short order. This is basically someone (me) who's had a few months of real training fighting someone who watched *Braveheart* a handful of times.

Allison enchants herself with defensive magic. No idea what she's doing other than creating shimmery lights around herself. Another ascendant trying to sneak Kingsley from behind notices Allison got loose and runs at her, hands up to claw her in the back of the head. No way in hell can she react in time to defend herself against one of these guys. I swat the redhead's next attack away hard enough to send her stumbling, then teleport between Allie and Mr. Skinny.

Damn good thing short hops are instant.

There's a reason it's a bad idea to try punching someone armed with a sword. As soon as his fist flashes at me, I instinctively parry... and lop the guy's arm off, about two inches in front of his elbow. The fist and forearm sail forward and bounce off Allison's shoulder. The guy shrieks in pain, gawking at the smoking stump while scrambling backward away from me. I thrust at his heart—but he's fast and my strike falls short of making contact.

Allison spins, apparently not realizing what hit her. She takes in the sight of me driving this guy off, then refocuses on Elizabeth and starts lobbing more fireballs.

An abnormally tall man with long brown hair comes out of nowhere, picks Kingsley up over his head in both hands, and hurls him at the wall—only he kinda misses, tossing the wolf through the doorway into the war room. A tremendous crash of splintering wood follows. Had to be the big table.

Oh, I guess they *do* have wood here. Must be expensive since it'd have to be transported from far off. The skinny ascendant gives the guy who threw him an annoyed look, then runs after Kingsley.

Tangent, Sam! comes Allison's thought.

Right. My bad.

Meanwhile, the tall guy also runs in after Kingsley. I have to believe my wolfish boyfriend can take care of himself in there. Too much going on out here...

Another exalted comes running down the hall, heading for me, but slashes at Allison on his way by. Light shimmers around her body, dramatically slowing the incoming blade to the point it grazes her arm rather than slices it off. I twist away from Skinny and punch the exalted in the face. He's surprisingly fast for basically a mortal, and manages to slice the outside of my left thigh before he goes flying away as an unconscious meat torpedo.

Maybe dead with a smashed face. I dunno. I'm kinda getting worried now and might've hit him harder than I wanted to.

Two more exalted run into the war room. Kingsley's growls sound entirely angry and not worried, so I'm going to continue trusting he has it handled.

Shit, this is rapidly getting out of control. I gotta end this fast or we're going to be overwhelmed.

The brute charges at me like a football line-backer, trying—once again—to bear-hug me. I'd say I dodge him like a matador evading a bull, but bullfighting is horrible and cruel. I don't feel at all guilty about stabbing this guy in the side as he goes by. Alas, he's too big and fast for me to score a kill shot, but he groans in pain.

The redheaded woman races up on my left side, slashing for my throat. I duck, punch her in the jaw with my sword hand, breaking it—her jaw, not my hand—launching her willowy body into the air. A red energy bolt flies under her, momentarily connecting Elizabeth's outstretched hand to my chest.

Her spell doesn't appear to cause any physical damage to my body, but it feels like I've been skinned, rolled in salt, and thrown in a giant deep fryer. Somehow, I keep myself from screaming since I know she'd adore hearing me suffer. Agony takes the strength out of my legs, dropping me to the floor in a sprawl. It occurs to me this feels exactly like being inside the guts of that massive demon-dragon. Is her spell tapping my memory of the most agony I've experienced?

The pain abruptly stops.

A shell of energy surrounds me, likely from Allison.

Relief from such horrid pain is so amazing, I go limp and fall on my face. Nice cold floor against my cheek. Ah...

The skinny ascendant grabs Allison and throws her—but she bounces off the wall like she's wrapped in bubble packing material, gliding gradually to a landing further down the hall. Unfortunately, she's right next to Elizabeth. Another unfortunately —I presently lack the ability to stand. The aftershock of such massive pain has my muscles on strike.

Dammit, I gotta do something!

Before Elizabeth can grab Allie, I teleport into the air above the bitch... and fall on her.

Instinctively, she catches me, momentarily stunned at having the falling object she sensed coming turn out to be me. Allison takes the opportunity of confusion to scramble back a few paces and summon an energy field on the floor beneath Elizabeth as she chucks me aside like an unwanted doll... Sparkling blue light forms a disc around her feet, though has no obvious effect beyond making her look down. According to Allie's thoughts, the magic is basically gluing Elizabeth's feet to the floor.

I pick myself up, shake off the last of the effect of the pain spell, and move to take advantage of the bitch being stuck—except the brutish ascendant grabs Allison. I redirect my charge at him instead, trying to chase him off her. He flings Allie aside, making no effort to defend his chest from my sword, and punches me right in the sternum.

The Devil Killer penetrates an inch or three into a body so damn dense it feels like I stabbed something slightly softer than a tree. My ribcage, on the other hand, is nowhere near as tough as this son of a bitch. Can't tell if only a spot in my sternum cracked, or if my entire ribcage split in half front-to-back. My turn to crash on the floor and go sliding. The stab wound I gave the brute ignites like a magnesium flare. He grimaces in pain, clamping his hand over it. My sword might not have landed a killing strike, but it's definitely crippled him even from such a shallow hit. Bringing my sword near their ascendant form is like waving filet mignon in front of a dog, only the Origin is the dog in this case. It *really* wants these bastards who have been eluding oblivion for so long to come home.

Tall Man flies out of the war room and smacks into the wall like one of those 'splat gummy' toys kids throw, sticking wherever they hit. His robes are shredded and bloody. At least one arm and both legs appear broken. He hangs there, stuck.

I lay still, waiting for my ribs to knit.

The redhead runs at me—but Kingsley dashes into the hall and bites the back of her dress, dragging her to a stop. Bare feet have zero traction on bloody stone floor. Evidently forgetting for the moment she's a powerful ascendant dark master, she screams like a horror movie victim as he drags her backward into the war room.

Elizabeth, seeming mildly perturbed, attempts to unstick her feet from the floor, largely ignoring the chaos around her.

Before me, the brute growls and raises a fist. As he does, a cloud of dark crimson fog forms around his hand, coalescing into a shiny snake seemingly made of blood. The instant it's completely solid, the serpent shoots forward like an arrow. Allison throws a counter-spell at him, causing the blood serpent to veer off course and hit the wall twenty feet past me rather than stab me in the heart. It splatters on contact.

Furious, the brute whirls on her. Allison raises both hands—and the big dude goes flying away as if caught in a category five hurricane existing only to him. Head over feet, he tumbles all the way to the end of the corridor, some thirty yards away, before smacking into a display stand holding a fancy suit of leather armor.

The redhead's screaming in the war room shifts from terror to anger. Kingsley snarls. Lots of banging and crashing follow. Tall guy finally peels off the wall and hits the floor. He's got the same expression on his face as I do. We end up looking at each other while waiting for our bones to knit.

"What are you even doing here?" wheezes Tall Guy in Pierre's voice.

Wow. Dude doesn't look like how Pierre sounded at all. I was expecting a little five-foot-two blonde guy. Not the complete opposite.

"I can't let her enslave an entire world," I say.

"Why do you care? It's not *your* world."

"Those who care about others only when they have a personal stake in the game are almost as evil as she is." I gasp at the pain of talking, but continue anyway. "Besides, I didn't come here to wipe out *all* dark masters, just to stop her from enslaving everyone here."

"We have lived in the shadows for far too long,"

rasps Pierre. "It is time for us to become true masters. I'm tired of hiding from the world. They *should* serve us."

"Seriously? Who cares about power? Is it really worth the headache of management?"

A heavy crash comes from the war room. Allison throws a spell on Elizabeth, wrapping her arms in blue energy ribbons, pinning them to her sides. I swear the bitch gives Allie an 'are you kidding' sneer before breaking out as easily as if she'd been tied with toilet paper.

Pierre winces as his left arm crunches back into place.

"Damn, I'm a little jealous," I say. "You guys heal way too fast."

He ignores me.

"Is it worth it?" I ask.

"Worth what?" snaps Pierre.

"Risking everything when the cost is being so close to oblivion?" A sharp *snap* comes from my ribcage. Oh, goodie. Guess the whole thing *didn't* break. That would've taken longer to mend. I sit up.

"You," snaps Elizabeth while glaring at Allison. "Make yourself useful."

Elizabeth's command to kill me overwhelms Allison's thoughts. I force myself up to my feet in time to dodge the first of her energy bolts, but she keeps chucking them at me. I feel like a damn Japanese Zero diving at an Allied warship through a hail of anti-aircraft fire. Allie's tennis-ball-sized energy bolts whiz past me one after another, close enough to set off tingles in my skin.

Elizabeth remains occupied, detangling herself from the sticky magic. The brute chases me around while I dodge fireballs. He's so big, he eats one or two, forcing Allison to slow down the barrage so she doesn't shred him. Another two exalted run into the fray, dragging me into a roving sword fight. They're much faster than a human but still can't keep up with me. They do land a few lucky scratches before I've wounded them too much to keep fighting.

Tammy's mental presence surges over the mind link from Allison, punting Elizabeth out of her head. Allison stops machine-gunning me and stares with an 'I'm *so* sorry' expression.

"Not your fault. I know what happened."

I stop short and spin on the brute, grabbing the Devil Killer in both hands and hacking as hard as my supernatural nature will let me swing at his left knee.

His body is incredibly tough. Still, I slice deep enough that his own weight and the momentum of him chasing me splinters his femur above the knee. He goes down hard, landing on his chin. I vault his sliding body and sprint for Elizabeth.

The crashing inside the war room is getting out of hand.

On my way past it, I peer in the door to see Kingsley caught in a fight against the redhead and two other ascendants. Elizabeth leaps out of the magical 'glue' patch, laughing at me as a group of exalted spills into the corridor from an archway, blocking me off. It pains me, but I can't allow my soft heart to doom this entire world, me, Kingsley, and Allison.

Doing my best to set emotion and guilt aside, I wade into the charging exalted. These men have obviously trained more at sword combat than I have, but the advantage in strength and speed is mine. I see them going for fancy moves and parries and can maneuver around them before their motions complete. Still, my attacks mostly sever limbs. I'm trying as much as I can not to kill any mortals.

So damn glad I found Sebastian. If I hadn't started training with him, I'd be having another Nordic zombie fight where all my effort went to defense. Exactly... not the most relaxing of vacations.

As I hack through the exalted, Elizabeth seems amused. Oh, that bitch. She's got to be toying with us. Maybe she finds it funny to force me to hurt innocent people. Each dark master who gets close to my sword seems to realize I hold their mortality in my hands. One bite from the blade is enough to convince most of them to play dead or get out of my way.

One guy, alas, has too much confidence in 'merely possessing' a human.

Sebastian's training causes my reflexes to move faster than my brain. Without thinking about it, a parry becomes a counterattack, stabbing a dude in the heart. Predictably, the mortal dies instantly...

and the Devil Killer eats the essence of the dark master who had been possessing him.

The sight of the glowing energy flowing into the blade finally puts a look of concern on Elizabeth's face. Yeah, she's not stupid. She knows if I get her with my sword before they have another Void made, her ass is going to merge back into the Origin. At least, I *think* this sword is an express train back to the hundredth dimension. Might be total oblivion, but really, what's the difference? Didn't Einstein say energy can neither be created nor destroyed? That'd have to count for souls too, so it must be Origin Express.

Another ascendant and more exalted throw themselves between me and Elizabeth. The ascendant doesn't seem too happy about it, almost as if Elizabeth is mind-controlling him.

"I'm not here to kill you all!" I shout. "I want only to stop her from destroying this world. Stand down and I will not hurt you."

The ascendant before me hesitates.

I leech psychic energy from the men in front of me, manufacturing a second wind and attacking in a surge. The exalted keep coming, relentless and mindless. What do the dark masters care if the human they're riding dies? I lop an exalted's hand off, parry two incoming sword strikes, and kick a guy in the face, knocking him back into the ranks behind him. I can't even tell where Allison went or how Kingsley's doing. Max said I only needed to keep Elizabeth occupied until they got here, but we're clearly losing now.

If I can end it, I have to.

I teleport past the mass of exalted to a spot beside Elizabeth.

As if expecting me to do exactly this, Elizabeth's already facing me when I appear. She thrusts her hand at me in a 'stop' gesture. The stone floor between us undulates like goopy mud, then stretches upward into a blunt-tipped spear, smashing me in the gut.

I fly backward off my feet, sailing butt-first through the air for a second before crashing to the floor and curling up in pain. Perhaps just witnessing a dark master die has affected Elizabeth's calm. She no longer appears to be blasé and confident. Mostly, she looks like bridezilla watching someone trash the wedding she'd planned to the tiniest detail… with a small trace of existential dread.

"I don't want to kill you," I rasp, cradling my gut. "Just swear you will not try to take over this world, and we can stop this."

"You don't learn," snarls Elizabeth. "You're going to keep following me forever. I'll never know peace."

"Hey, now you know how I've felt for the past, oh, fourteen years." I pull myself up to my feet. "Can we stop this idiocy? You have immortality and power already. Do you really need to rule over normal humans?"

"You know nothing of power!" shouts Elizabeth —right before throwing a lightning bolt at me.

I dive into a somersault, narrowly avoiding a thick, serpentine shaft of white-hot electricity that sears a jagged black stain into the stone. The *bang* is louder than a shotgun.

Some vampires, especially older ones, think of humans the way humans think of cows: livestock for food. Then you have ones like Elizabeth. She thinks of humans more like grapes, as in, more insignificant than even animals.

Enraged—and perhaps reminded I possess the ability to destroy her permanently—Elizabeth goes into a frenzy of chucking lightning bolts at me. The amount of mental energy I inhale to empower myself from the nearby exalted knocks four of them out cold. Despite accelerating myself to the upper limit of my abilities, I'm forced to run away down the hall to have any chance of dodging the rapid-fire barrage of lightning coming from Elizabeth.

A number of exalted give chase.

The next lightning bolt strikes four of them, knocking them flat—dead or unconscious I can't quite tell. Kingsley the wolf comes flying out of the war room, hits the wall, and lands in the corridor, favoring his two left legs. The brute blurs after him, appearing almost like a teleportation beside him, ramming his falchion into Kingsley's side.

The giant wolf groans and slumps into a heap, no longer moving. He rapidly shifts back to human form.

"I despise werewolves," says the brute, in Dormund's voice.

I begin to thrust my sword at an imaginary opponent, teleporting beside Elizabeth in mid-attack. The Devil Killer's tip pierces her left shoulder from behind; she spins to her right, letting the blade slip out of her and go past. I barely manage to swing the blade down to catch her caustic scimitar, stopping it before it bites into my stomach. She's got the fear of death in her eyes.

Self-preservation wins out.

Frantic, she flicks her hand at me, summoning a wave of invisible force that knocks me staggering away. Pierre, the redhead, and the skinny man all surround me, attacking. Swords are everywhere. It's all I can do to keep parrying. Realizing I've got seconds left before one of them gets the upper hand, I teleport back to Elizabeth. My sudden absence causes Skinny and the redhead to stab each other.

I appear right in the path of a lightning bolt flying from Elizabeth's outstretched fingers.

Too late, I realize she's reading my mind. Teleporting at her is basically giving her a free shot on me because she knows exactly where I'm going to appear. Since she's become afraid for her existence, the gloves are off.

I'd say the lightning hurts, but it kinda doesn't. My whole body goes numb and loses control. I flop to the floor, twitching like a tuna on the deck of a fishing boat. Tiny sparks crackle up and down my limbs, a stinging army of electric fire ants sizzling. My body refuses to respond to my brain. Electricity overwhelms my nerves. I can't feel anything more than the zapping, nor can I move.

Redhead, Skinny, and Pierre hurry over to surround me.

Shit. Not good. At least since I'm momentarily paralyzed, they are content to gloat for now.

Allison—somewhere out of my sight—emits a bark like a kicked chicken. Our mind link tells me she lost consciousness. It didn't drop, though. No idea why they didn't kill her, but I'm not gonna question it. Small favors.

"I grow tired of Samantha's interference." Elizabeth sighs in a way like she's being forced to break a friendship because I've gone just a little too far. Sorry, lady, but we didn't have a friendship. "End it. And use that irritating sword of hers. I do not want her coming back."

"With pleasure," says the redhead.

With every ounce of determination I have, I clench my grip on the Devil Killer's handle—but she plucks my fingers away like limp hot dogs and picks up my sword.

"Ooh, this is pretty. I love black." Smoke wafts from under her grip. "Ouch. Guess it doesn't like me back. Suppose I should get this over with quick before my hand's on fire." She points my sword at my face. "Bye."

I scream inside my head, ordering my body to move.

But the only thing my muscles want to do is twitch.

Chapter Fourteen
Too Late For Me

The redhead slides her foot under my shoulder and kicks me over onto my back, exposing my heart. She gives me this patronizing little smile.

My body still doesn't want to move. Shit! I think of my kids and send a thought of 'I'm sorry,' bracing for my express train to oblivion. Redhead draws her arm back to thrust the blade—*my* blade— the sword Azrael gave me, into my heart.

Azrael.

Angels.

Wait!

My body isn't moving, but my wings aren't made of meat.

It's a little cramped in this corridor to stretch them out, but I'm not trying to fly. My wings bursting out of my back props my limp body up a little. Redhead pauses, caught off guard by the bizarre sight. I'd grin if my face was capable of it, but alas, no. Channeling the power Azrael gave me, I command the wings to glow as they did back in Alaska, focusing a brilliant sunbeam down the hall, mostly on the redhead.

She recoils, shielding her eyes. The light hurts her, but the ascendant have beat the sun thing, too. Not a surprise, the guy grabbed the creator, Zandra, in broad daylight and didn't seem the least bit distressed.

Pins and needles wash over me. Lightning sparks snap from my hands to the floor, the paralyzing charge from Elizabeth's spell grounding out of me at last. I roll forward to my feet, grab the Devil Killer from the distracted woman, and swing for her neck. She can't see in the glare, offering no defense. My strike is clean. Her head falls to the floor, trailed by a long ribbon of red hair.

Dammit. I reacted by reflex, not thinking. Beheading her won't send her back to the Origin. Gotta hit her in the heart. I recover from the grand slam decapitating swing and start to thrust at her defenseless body—when another lightning bolt from Elizabeth strikes me in the torso.

I stop sliding a few feet away, smoke rising from my once-again paralyzed body.

Oh, I'm really starting to freakin' hate lightning.

Elizabeth laughs, casually raising her hand to feed me another one.

A glowing yellow energy bolt from behind blows out Elizabeth's left knee. She rocks back, arms flinging up—and the second lightning bolt passes over me instead of going up my nose. Growling, Elizabeth glares at me as if to say 'you can wait a moment.'

She extends her fangs and turns to face Allison. "I'm not going to kill you. No, I have something better planned."

Skinny and Pierre blur, appearing on either side of Allie in a fraction of a second, grabbing her arms. She kicks, struggling to escape, but mortal strength doesn't move the two ascendants holding her.

Elizabeth saunters over to Allison and traces a fingertip down her cheek. "I think I'm going to take you for my own. Another witch out of the cycle. You will serve me as a vampire. Yes… your combination of psychic talents and magic will serve me quite nicely. I'm afraid you will need to be kept in shackles until the dark master has full control."

"Fuck you." Allison spits at her. "I'm stronger than you think. You're going to be waiting a long damn time."

"Time is meaningless to me." Elizabeth leans in as if to bite her on the neck.

Allison struggles to get away, screaming, "Sam!"

By sheer force of determination to protect my friend, I force myself to move despite the paralyzing magic. It feels as if my muscles are peeling apart. With all the grace of a drunk zombie, I sway to my feet... and summon a fireball of my own. Compared to the masters of magic around me, my attempt is pathetic at best. But it does the trick, smacking into the back of Lizzy's head as surely as if I had slapped her with an open palm.

Growling, she pulls her face away from Allison's still-untouched neck. But instead of turning towards me, she looks down an intersecting corridor —and flings herself back as a silver crossbow quarrel flies through the space where her head was a second before.

Bright orange light floods the hallway. Pierre and Skinny continue holding Allison, though they make 'WTF' faces into the branching corridor. The reason for their expressions appears soon after— The Fire Warrior.

Anthony strides up to Pierre, raising a broadsword surrounded in a glowing halo of golden light. Where the hell did that sword come from? Pierre lets go of Allison's arm, diving out from under the first attack—but not in time. Anthony's sword cuts him in half from shoulder to groin, leaving both pieces engulfed in fire.

Pierre—still apparently alive despite being severed vertically—screams in agony, his pieces twitching. Skinny lets go of Allison and runs away. Pierre stops screaming. White glowing light rises from the smoldering remains, racing off into the distance and upward.

Hmm, okay. Anthony's sword didn't suck up the ghost vapors like mine does. Guess Elizabeth is right about returning to the whole fifth dimension thing. Light Warriors charge in behind Anthony.

Dormund backs up, raising his arms in a feeble defense as a barrage of silver-tipped crossbow quarrels strike him all over the head and chest. They barely pierce in enough to stick, though seem to be rather painful. The Fire Warrior strides toward him. Dormund roars a war shout and charges. For reasons I cannot explain, the sight of such a big, muscular ascendant vampire trying to kill my son *doesn't* fill me with panic. It's no more stressful than watching him go against a meaner kid in sports. A group of Light Warriors spill into the hallway, most hastily reloading their crossbows, except for Yasmeen and Olivia who clutch glowing crystals in each hand.

Elizabeth thrusts her hands straight up.

Allison, Yasmeen, and Olivia all do something magic at her at the same time.

Suddenly, our surroundings change from a fairly tight corridor to the huge open courtyard across the street from the castle entrance. We've all teleported out of the castle. Elizabeth, wide-eyed, looks around with a manic expression. The bitch definitely didn't expect to do this. Allison's thinking she tried to teleport across the world, fleeing. It appears the Light Warrior mystics interfered with the teleportation spell, redirecting it to the courtyard and expanding the magic to grab everyone within 200 feet.

A chaotic mess of true vampires—obvious since they're already catching fire from being out in the sun—exalted, ascendant dark masters, Light Warriors, and a few ordinary soldiers erupt in a frenzy of fighting since no walls, stairs, or doors are in the way anymore. Allison giggles inside her head at seeing the exalted and true vamps, because 'vampires come in both smoking and non-smoking varieties.'

Ugh.

Yasmeen, Olivia, and Madelyn focus on Elizabeth while chanting magically. Nothing obvious happens, though the fear in Elizabeth's eyes hints they might be doing something to stop her from teleporting again. She points at them. Several ascendant dark masters and numerous exalted all rush at the three women.

The Fire Warrior sprouts bright white wings, also wreathed in fire, and fly-leaps to stand in front of them. Say what? When the hell did he get wings?

Not sure they came from hell, thinks Allison. I sense her winking.

Will figure it out later. No time to worry about my son sprouting extra body parts right now. I rush across the courtyard toward Elizabeth, fighting my way through exalted and true vampires. The vamps are pretty freakin' worthless out here in the sun. This is exactly why my staying in HUD would've been a horrible idea. In the light of day, vamps are mostly blind and have the reaction time of senior citizens overdosed on valium.

I try to finish off the true vamps with thrusts to the heart as often as possible. The exalted, I mostly punch, backhand, or kick out of my way. The ascendants are ripping into the Light Warriors pretty bad. Even with their magical boosts, the dark masters in a pure physical form are just too damn powerful for mortal humans to deal with.

The Fire Warrior plays goalie for the three mystics, cutting down ascendant and true vampires with relative ease. The ascendants claw or stab him a few times, but superficially. Whenever he gets his hands on an exalted, Anthony grabs them by the throat, holds them up for a few seconds, then throws them aside... the wispy black energy of a departing dark master soul gliding away.

What the frick? How is he de-possessing them like that?

Not gonna argue. Damn neat trick, though.

Not a trick, Mom, says Tammy in my head. *I'll explain later. Just please stay alive!*

Planning on it.

I throw myself into a tangle of ascendants, Light Warriors, and Elizabeth near the center of the courtyard. She's still trying to do something magical, either throw more lighting, mind control people, or teleport away, but it's not working too well. She does fire off a few lightning zaps, but they're far less intense than the ones she hit me with earlier and don't paralyze anyone. Of course, she is blowing arms and legs off Light Warriors, so paralysis might be difficult to judge.

My fingers go numb from the relentless shock of my sword smashing into other swords. I lose track of the number of superficial wounds, and not-so-superficial wounds hitting me. I'm still moving, so none of them can be *too* bad, right? Meanwhile, exalted and ascendant drop off to either side. I'm making headway.

Finally, I get close enough to attack Elizabeth directly and leap into a lunging thrust for her heart. An ascendant swats my blade down so it pierces Elizabeth's hip instead. The Light Warrior he'd been fighting stabs him in the back with a silver-edged sword. Damn fool. Lowered his guard to protect Elizabeth.

She slashes at me, roaring in a blind rage. She's so damn angry, her skill's gone into the toilet but she's also effing strong. It's a damn good thing my sword is angelic metal or it would snap under the forces released each time our blades crash together. Sparks and acid fly again and again. I need to grab my sword in both hands to keep hold of it, lest she swat it right out of my grip.

"Stop trying to take over this world and we don't have to fight," I yell.

She slashes at my head.

I duck, pop up, and thrust for her chest again.

She scoops her blade under mine, lifting it away, razor edges scraping in a painful nails-on-chalkboard way. "This world is mine, Samantha! You are too late to change anything. Your precious Light Warriors are dying, and for what? A momentary delay. You've killed them all, Sam. You brought them here. This world was none of their concern."

Kingsley zooms by in a streak of black fur. Whew. Gotta love werewolf healing. I think he wants some revenge, since he appears to be focusing on true vampires who make for easy pickings. Some run for the cover of darkness inside the castle.

Dillon charges Elizabeth from the left. She senses him coming, spinning into a slash across his chest. The attack is so blindingly fast, he couldn't react to defend himself. He staggers, screaming past a clenched jaw at the pain of acid eating away at his insides. Elizabeth moves to follow up, intent on taking his head off—I lunge forward to defend him. She hacks down into my right knee, the killing strike on Dillon a fake.

Ooh, bitch.

My right leg gives out, dumping me onto the wounded knee.

Yes, falling with all my weight onto a half-cut-through knee is uncomfortable.

Elizabeth swings down at my head—her blade hits another with a loud *clang.*

I cringe a bit at the noise and peer up at a gleaming silver falchion above my head, holding Elizabeth's blade at bay.

"Mother…" Max pushes Elizabeth's scimitar away from me, forcing her back a step and putting himself between us. "Why are you doing this? Did you not learn anything from your centuries in the Void?"

"Archibald…" Elizabeth sighs. "You are still a disappointment, refusing to claim the power that is rightfully yours."

I grit my teeth, forcing myself upright, all my weight on my left leg. No, I do not like the sensation of my right shin and foot dangling.

"Mother," says Max. "I have never given up hope the day will come when you return to the light."

They stare at each other for a few seconds as screams, roaring fireballs, and death surround us on all sides.

"You always were an idealistic fool." Elizabeth sneers. "Together, we could have been unstoppable. If not for you, the world would have been a vastly different place. *This* world is even better than the one you call home. Magic is so much more here."

"It wasn't too late for me, Mother. It does not have to be too late for you."

Elizabeth looks down, tears gathering in the corners of her eyes. "That life is over for us. Would you think less of me if I admitted I missed it? You were such a bright, happy boy."

"I would not think less of you for that, no, Mother. There are none who are beyond redemption." Max reaches to her. "Our goal is not to destroy you. I want to save you."

Elizabeth sniffles, dabbing tears. She cringes away, ashamed. "After everything, you don't despise me?"

Max… don't believe it. She's bullshitting you.

I grasp his shoulder with my left hand.

"How could I despise my own mother?"

"Even after what I did to you?"

"Even then. You are my mother." Max smiles. "Take my hand. We have much to do."

Elizabeth looks up, her tearful expression heavy with surprise. She steps close as if to hug Max.

… and thrusts her caustic scimitar at his chest.

I expected it. I knew the bitch was lying. But she's freakin' *fast.*

Simultaneously, I yank Max away from her while thrusting the Devil Killer at Elizabeth's heart.

For an instant that feels like a minute, the three of us stand there in a macabre tangle. My sword impaled through her chest, her sword impaling Max, though not in the heart. Me standing there stunned at having hit Elizabeth at all. It's… almost as if she let me.

"Such an idealist…" whispers Elizabeth. "It is too late for me."

Max collapses over backward, cradling his gut.

Elizabeth's sword slips out of her grasp and clatters to the stone. She throws her head back, arms out to either side. Spirit energy wells up out of the earth, whirling into a cyclone of glowing strands filling the courtyard. Pottery shatters at random. The exalted still on their feet blow over in the fierce, whipping wind. Kingsley stops chasing vampires and hunkers down to resist the gale.

Allison clings to Yasmeen, Olivia, and Madelyn.

Cracks race over Elizabeth's body, revealing black vapor inside, as though she'd been a hollow porcelain shell full of shadows. Her expression of contentment is eerie. After all this, so many years, centuries even, what made her simply stand there? Did Max really distract her enough for me to land a strike, or did she give up and let me hit her? Is she expecting to go to the fifth dimension? Abandoning her plan to take over this world to resume plotting in the shadows somewhere?

If so, I think she's wrong.

In that moment, she knows she's wrong too. The look of contentment turns into one of terror and fear... and finally... peace.

My sword shudders in my grasp.

Elizabeth's physical body explodes into a blast of wind and smoke, joining the cyclone battering the courtyard. Multiple threads of glowing energy connect the storm to my sword. The Devil Killer shakes like a giant is trying to wrench it away from me. It soon heats to the point my hands feel ready to catch fire.

I can't tell if it's absorbing her soul or merely touching it. For what feels like minutes, every ounce of my concentration is spent trying to keep the sword from flying out of my hands. So much power roars around me, I fear the sword will fly into outer space if I lose my grip. A sudden explosion goes off in the air in front of me, slapping me flat to the ground.

She's gone. Back to the source. I know this much is true.

Above me, cloudless blue sky.

Around me, silence.

Inside me, pain.

After a moment of lying there enjoying the quiet, the scent of burned stone makes me turn my head to the right, staring down the length of my arm at my sword. Courtyard tiles have become magma under the Devil Killer's blade. Whoa.

Hey, at least it's quiet.

The fighting's stopped.

Chapter Fifteen
Warrior of Light

Max gurgles.

I roll onto all fours and crawl to him.

Blood bubbles out of his mouth on each breath, coating his chin and dripping onto his chest. The wound appears mortal but not immediately fatal. It's unreal to see this man, Archibald Maximus, the immortal alchemist I've come to think of as a close friend, almost brother... damn near close to death. Throughout the supernatural oddity my life has become, he's been there as a source of reassurance, comfort, wisdom. Even though he looks younger than me, his *presence* is old.

Seeing him minutes from death is so damn surreal...

This is the moment the phrase 'I can't even' finally makes sense to me.

Reflexively, I try to staunch the bleeding as

much as I can, even though it's pointless. We're in a world so primitive they don't even have surgical tools. The best doctor they have here isn't going to be able to do anything to fix this. Desperately, I hold pressure on the wound while tears stream down my face. My voice won't cooperate to tell him how much he means to me.

Could turning him into a vampire work? I have no idea if it's even something within my power to do anymore. My vampirism has nothing to do with blood, fangs, or biting—so even if I *could* do it, the mechanism of *how* is a blank. And I don't have a dark master inside me. Pretty sure that's a require-ment to pass on the curse. Not to mention Max would refuse. He's spent his life fighting the dark masters. He'd never want one inside him.

Futility builds until I find myself crying in silence.

Seconds later, a rush of sound reaches me—along with loud sobbing. The remaining Light War-riors pursue a handful of ascendants beyond the castle. Oh, it hadn't become silent. I momentarily went deaf. Again. The sobbing is coming from me.

"Sam," rasps Max.

"I'm here…"

He smiles up at me. "Don't mourn my passing. I have had more life than anyone has a right to. I am at peace. Finally, we have stopped her. After so long…" He closes his eyes. "I expected she would take me with her."

"Is this where I'm supposed to say something

cheesy like you still have a lot to live for?"

He grunts. "Don't make me laugh. I'd ask you to hurry this along, but I don't wish to be killed by that blade of yours."

"I could never..."

Max looks up at me. "You are upset."

"Of course I'm upset. You're dying! Did you forget I have like two friends and you're one of them?" I keep trying to hold back the blood leaking from the gaping wound in his abdomen.

The flutter of fire in the wind approaches.

I look up at my son, rather the Fire Warrior— now with wings.

"Max," says Anthony.

At least, it sounds like my son's voice... mostly. It's his voice run through electronics to make it sound deeper, with a little reverb. Okay, since when does the Fire Warrior talk?

Apparently, since now, thinks Allison. *Hey, is the bitch gone?*

Yes, I think.

"Is it time?" asks Max, looking at the Fire Warrior.

"It is not time for you to return to the Origin." My son rests his large, flaming hand on Max's gut wound. Golden light wells up beneath his fingers.

All the tension in Max's body evaporates. He sags limp on the ground, but doesn't lose consciousness. "This is... unexpected."

Anthony removes his hand, revealing a small bruise on Max's stomach where a huge gash had been.

"Umm, Ant? You can heal? Since when?"

The Fire Warrior looks at me. "Since now, Ma."

"What happened to you?"

"Actually, it started a long time ago."

"It's so weird seeing him talk," says Allison. "And how does he sound like Anthony when he's the Fire Warrior?"

My son looks around the courtyard. "Give me a sec, Ma."

I sit there on the ground beside Max, leaning on Allison. Even my hair hurts right now. Allison cringes, but pushes past her squeamishness to reposition the lower half of my right leg so it heals faster.

"Ouch. Thanks."

Anthony walks around the courtyard, healing Light Warriors who fell but didn't die, starting with Dillon.

Allison gives me side eye. *Why didn't he heal you?*

I'm guessing he probably can't because it's not necessary. I can sorta put myself back together.

Oh. That makes sense.

"You're probably wondering what happened to him," whispers Max. He sounds exhausted, more than trying to keep quiet. "He's an angel, in case you didn't know."

"She's been calling him that ever since he was born," says Allison. "How many kids do you know who are *that* polite, respectful, and obedient?"

"Max is being literal, Allie. I think my kid literally got his wings." I'm about to burst into tears since it likely means he died out there, but for some reason, I don't. It hits me that he died almost nine years ago. An immortal with no dark master... he'd become an angel as soon as I'd reversed the vampirism on him. Does my son sprouting wings mean he's going to have to go away?

I squeeze Allison.

She gurgles. *Little tight, Sam. Unlike some people, I need to breathe.*

Hey, I need to breathe again, too. Just can hold my breath for a really long time.

Holy shit. Your sword's melting into the ground.

I look over at the Devil Killer. It's melted through the three-inch-thick paver stones to the earth below, and is *still* kinda glowing orange.

"Why is it doing that?" asks Allison.

"I think it ate Elizabeth."

Max exhales. "It sent her where she belongs. Where I should be."

"Apparently not." Allison pats him on the head. "Otherwise, Anthony wouldn't have been able to fix you."

Kingsley trots over and collapses in a furry heap next to us. He's totally got a 'screw this, I'm going to sleep for a week' vibe.

"Are you sure it's not this world's much looser grip of magic having that effect on Anthony?" I ask. "Maybe whatever powers he has are spreading out beyond their normal boundaries here?"

Allison shrugs. "We'll find out as soon as we go home."

"Should I be thrilled or panicking that my son's apparently an angel?"

Allison nudges me. "How about proud?"

Chapter Sixteen
Monkeys

We gather ourselves in the furthest corner of the courtyard, tending to the wounded.

Max thinks the remaining ascendants as well as the true vampires might come after us once the sun goes down—which is going to happen in about an hour. We don't see any sign of vampires, exalted, or any sign Elizabeth herself had ever been here.

A short while later, the roar of hundreds of shouting voices spill down the street.

What the hell?

Curious, I get up and walk toward the noise. Oh, goody. My leg is solid again. Allison follows.

The commotion is coming not far past the castle, in what appears to be the city's 'main drag.' Except the main drag is now a battleground. Soldiers wearing the colors of Elizabeth's forces (black and red) clash with soldiers in the brown leather of the former king's army. The two forces don't appear to be going after each other in *too* much of a frenzy at least.

The men and women on 'team Elizabeth' aren't giving off the sense of being mind-controlled, merely loyal to (or terrified of) their empress.

"Is this where you hold up her severed head and tell them it's over?" asks Allison.

"Nah. Not my circus. Not my monkeys. Mortals fighting mortals isn't our problem."

"This wouldn't be happening if not for Elizabeth," says Anthony right behind us.

I nearly jump out of my skin.

My son always did find it hilarious to sneak up on me or Tammy. Who thought it a good idea to give the boy angelic powers? I peer back at him. Despite still mostly looking like the Fire Warrior, he's smirking the same way he usually does whenever he startles us.

"He's got a point." Allison nods. "But there's a small problem. Elizabeth didn't leave behind a severed head. She kind of exploded into glowing plasma. Umm, I could maybe try to conjure one?"

Anthony raises both eyebrows. Fiery eyebrows, mind you.

"Nah. They won't fall for it," I say, then stare at the humans fighting for a few seconds. Such stupidity. "Oh. Wait. Idea."

Eyes closed, I summon the single flame and picture the inn room where I left Fahma, Nahari, and the four former bath attendant slaves. Through the tiny flickering light, I see six women still in the room. The area by the door is open, so I aim there and move toward the fire even as it comes to me.

All six women jump when I appear out of thin air.

They've traded their illusionary clothes for real ones, dressed like any other woman of middling social class in the city. The four former slaves all seem on edge, giving off a sense like criminals about to be caught by the police. Queen Fahma and her daughter, Nahari, are also frightened; then again, they've been expecting to face execution.

"Sorry that took so long," I say. "Was a bit more of a struggle than I expected. Long story short... Queen Fahma, would you like your throne back?"

She stares at me, stunned. "It's impossible. That woman is... a goddess."

"In her own mind, yes. But she is gone now."

"You speak the truth?"

I slip into her mind and replay my own memory of Elizabeth dying at the end of my sword, her soul returning to the Origin.

"You *do* speak the truth." She begins to bow, thinking me the new empress.

"Whoa. No. I want to return the throne to you, but I have one condition."

"Yes, anything."

"Make slavery illegal," I say.

Nahari perks up, grabbing the queen by the arm. "Yes, Mother! Do as she asks."

Queen Fahma blinks, her brain stuck on the

memory I'd played for her. Also, she'd probably expected me to ask for personal gain. "I agree to your terms. I had a taste of slavery. It is... barbaric."

The four other women exchange glances, then stare wide-eyed at Fahma like they can't believe what they're hearing.

"Excellent. Gotta borrow you real quick. Your people need you. Now!" I grab Fahma and Nahari's hands—then teleport back to the street by Allison and Anthony.

Both women emit yelps of surprise.

I point at the war on the street before us. "Queen Fahma, your throne is once again yours. Elizabeth is destroyed. It seems as though some of your soldiers are wearing the wrong uniform and fighting for the wrong side." I turn to my witchy friend. "Allison, help us out here?"

Reading my intent, she throws a magical flare into the sky. It flies up, emitting a screeching wail like a firework before exploding with a cannon-like *boom.*

The soldiers mostly all stop what they're doing to flinch, and peer up in confusion.

"Stop fighting each other," I shout. "The tyrant empress is dead. Behold, your rightful queen." I gesture at Fahma.

"Is this real?" whispers Fahma.

"Yep. Your house had a rat problem. It's clean now." I bite my lip. "Well, clean is relative. Some-one's going to need to scrape up the bodies, but they're dead. Well, most of them. The others are on the run."

The soldiers stare at the queen and her daughter. It takes them a painfully long time to recognize them in ordinary clothing, but one by one, realization sets in. Those in the brown armor erupt in joyous cheers while the ones in Elizabeth's colors appear more bewildered, gradually realizing her voice in their heads has stopped.

Queen Fahma approaches the army, ordering them to stop killing each other immediately. Those wearing Elizabeth's colors strip down immediately. Soon, they stand there in what looks like long underwear.

Good.

Our work here is done.

We head back toward the courtyard, but encounter the Light Warriors and Kingsley coming our way. Max seems in much better spirits already, no longer seeming like he would've preferred to be dead. Guess most people would be heartbroken if their mother tried to kill them, but he's used to it. I kinda know how he feels. No, my mother would never have actively try to hurt me, but the two of us aren't close. A betrayal from her wouldn't hurt me as much as it would hurt someone with a normal family relationship to have their mother turn on them.

On the walk back out of Iskariya to the tent city, I fill Max in on the situation with the queen and how it appears things here in this kingdom will recover from Elizabeth's interference without *too* much disruption.

"Oh, before I forget. She dispatched vampires to the other cities to mind control the dukes," I say. "Not sure if she sent vampires or ascendants. I probably ought to warn the queen."

"Mardat is already working on this intelligence," says Max. "Tammy relayed the contents of what the three of you eavesdropped on. Tuns out the folk here have these small orbs that allow them to communicate between cities. The spy network in the other cities is aware vampire agents are on the way."

"Oh, great." I smile. "Less work for us. Can we go home now?"

"I believe so." Max looks at the watch he isn't wearing. "Might even make it in time for Conan."

Okay, I *almost* laugh. Still kinda emotionally tattered from almost watching him die… and worrying what's going on with Anthony.

We arrive at the big tent—and find it empty.

"Tam?" I ask.

Anthony, back to his normal size and holding a cloth around his waist, scurries into the tent. "She probably went looking for somewhere to pee." He ducks behind a partition to put a tunic on.

It's a good thing my hippie brother Clayton didn't turn into a werewolf, a Fire Warrior, or get a friend like Talos. It would've been the last straw to make him give up on clothing entirely.

Oh, good, you guys are done and I can stop being derpy now, says Tammy in my head.

Actually, she speaks in everyone's heads since they all react to her.

Little help, guys?

I blink. Help? What happened?

Oh, nothing much. Got kidnapped by slavers. I'm sitting in a big cage with some other women. Can't see much 'cause I'm blindfolded and they tied my hands.

My blood boils.

Chill, Mom. No one like did anything creepy... yet. Came out of the trance in here like this.

"Crap!" yells Anthony. "I wanted to stay here with her, but it felt like I needed to help you guys at the castle or something truly bad would happen. Max wasn't quite ready for the frontal assault, but I went anyway."

"You *were* needed there," I say in a grim tone. "Tammy's fine. If you stayed here, you'd have prevented them from abducting her, but we wouldn't have beaten Elizabeth."

Mom? Can you maybe like hurry up? I'm only gonna stay calm for like another twenty minutes before I start freaking out. Oh, and before they auction me off. No way!

No way, what? I ask.

They're practically auctioning me off for free! They think I'm weak and sickly because I'm so pale and regret kidnapping me. The nerve!

Despite myself, I laugh. Oh, they're going to regret it alright. Be right there.

Chapter Seventeen
Not For Sale

Kingsley sniffs the ground.

Honestly, I probably could too, but there are far too many scents here for a human brain to process individually. The big wolf takes off at a brisk trot. Dealing with a bunch of mortals isn't a problem for us, so Max and his people go in a different direction to finish recovering the bodies of their fallen.

Crap! Mom! yells Tammy again. *They opened our cell. Someone's grabbing my arm.*

We're coming. Won't be long. Hold it together, okay?

Kingsley breaks into a run.

Wait, Tam... you can feel where my brain is, right?

Yeah, she replies, a nervous tremble in her telepathic voice.

I extend my wings and leap into the air. Flying

at 120 is faster than a giant wolf with his nose to the ground. Which way, kiddo?

Okay, you're going kinda off to the side. Turn left a little.

I enter a gradual turn.

Stop! You're coming right toward me now.

It's the same slave market we saw earlier. It sits at the end of a street with walls on three sides. Queen Fahma is going to outlaw slavery, but if government here is anything like our world, it's going to take years before all the slaves are free. And there's no damn way anyone is putting a collar on either one of my kids. Of course, I doubt anyone could put one on Anthony.

After circling, I slow to a hover. Aha! Tammy's standing on a raised platform in a line with other captives, behind another young woman. Two abducted men are behind my daughter, then another three girls who appear even younger, mid-teens. All the captives' hands are bound behind their backs with rope.

Another woman, early twenties, stands near the center of the stage, with only a scrap of fabric around her. The man who appears to own the slave business is looking her over the way one might study a horse.

The slavers consist of eleven men: one guy in a rich white robe, plus ten seedy-looking individuals brandishing swords, who are acting as guards and 'wranglers.' Two sets of cages stand on either side of the stage, containing a mix of men and women.

I swoop straight down onto the stage and land in front of the 'merchant.'

"You abducted my daughter," I say, then draw the Devil Killer. "I'll give you once chance to run."

The men look at their rich leader. To help influence their decision, I sprout my wings again, stretching them far and wide... and the men all scramble over each other, each more desperate than the other to get the hell out of there. I chuckle as half of them fall off the stage. Their scrambling soon turns into outright running. Some turn back and look at me... and run faster.

I rush over to Tammy and carefully slice the rope off her wrists.

She rips the blindfold off and clamp hugs me. I comfort her as she lets emotion leak from her eyes. She's not crying per se, just overwhelmed. "You're safe, sweetie."

"Ugh, that sucked! I was so focused on shield-ing you guys from Elizabeth, I didn't even realize anyone grabbed me until I was already in a damn cage. Sorry I let her get Allison for a few minutes. Elizabeth is really damn strong."

"Was," I say. "And Anthony's really sorry, too."

She nods. "Yeah, I know. Oh... uhh, Mom, he thinks he saw the Archangel Michael."

"Yeah. He most likely did. Wasn't a hallucina-tion."

"Whoa." Tammy blinks, staring at me for a moment while looking at my memories. "Holy crap, the big guy talked?"

"Yeah, shocked me, too."

Tammy gets her breathing under control. "I think that woman is wondering if we're going to leave her tied up all day. She's also wondering why you have wings and if you're going to kill her."

I glance at the woman who'd been in the middle of her 'appraisal' when I landed. "Of course not. They took my daughter, but I'm here to help all of you."

I grab a convenient knife off the floor and slice the ropes off the woman's wrists. Using the Devil Killer to cut ropes off people is a bit much—and dangerous considering the blade tends to ignite things. After I cut her loose, she calmly picks up the dress she'd been wearing before and puts it on. I make my way down the line, cutting everyone loose. Most of them run off after thanking me. They're expecting the soldiers to swoop in at any minute, and want to be far away from here before they end up being forced back into captivity.

Kingsley, Anthony, and Allison arrive at the other end of the alley. Soon, we're trashing the slaver's 'shop,' breaking the cages open and snapping collars off the people inside them. None of the people in the cages are physically restrained beyond the cell, only stuck in enchanted collars… which are more like a heavy jewelry item than a leash, at least in a physical sense.

With one exception, the children who'd been enslaved were sold by their parents due to extreme poverty. I try not to let myself become insanely pissed at the idea. After all, slavery in this world doesn't necessarily mean horrible abuse, more of a low social standing and forced labor. Still. Children need to be children, not workers. I know, different society, it's not my place to tell anyone what's 'moral,' but dammit. Screw this place. I'm not Captain Kirk. I *will* interfere with other societies.

With Tammy safe and Anthony here to keep an eye on things, I spend like an hour ferrying kids back to their parents and putting the fear of hell into them. Well, it's more like giving them a scare and a mental compulsion never to do anything like that again—and to protect their kids.

Ugh, this place. I can't wrap my head around those parents thinking their children's lives would be *improved* as someone's property. Even in an alternate world, the wealthy have managed to brainwash normal people into believing they're better off being owned than being poor.

The one exception, a boy of about seven named Mahdi, had no parents to sell him. He's a street waif living off whatever he can steal and beg for. Apparently, being a starving child is still not permission to steal—even bread—since this place is so adamant about thievery being a horrid crime. The soldiers dragged him here and gave him to the slavers as punishment for taking food.

Again, 'ugh, this place.'

Easy enough to fix even if I am ignoring any semblance of ethics.

I fly around carrying him for a little while until he spots a friendly seeming couple in their early thirties. They appear to own a garment shop, so are probably at least middle class. After confirming the addition of a child to their lives won't unduly burden them, I 'encourage' them to take Mahdi in and raise him as their own.

Okay. My work here is done. Time to go home.

Chapter Eighteen
A Final Thorn

We make a brief stop at the tent to collect our 'modern world' clothes. Since it really doesn't matter now if we stand out, we change back into them. One of the waiting alchemists leads us into the desert to a spot where Max and the other the Light Warriors are preparing the portal.

One problem with tracing glyphs in desert sand: they don't last long. The symbols they made to bring everyone in before the attack on the castle have already disappeared. As the mystics start to chant, Anthony moves close, staring at the spot where the portal will appear. Oh, wow. I wonder if he had any effect on it before. Could he have been doing some kind of angel stuff without even realizing he could? Max *did* seem mildly surprised they got the portal to work on the first try.

A spot of glowing orange appears in midair

about five feet off the ground. It expands outward to a ten-foot circle the color of raw scrambled eggs. Snaps of lightning race around the edge for a few seconds before the interior pulls inward, stretching into a golden-walled tunnel with the Venezuelan jungle on the other side.

Awesome.

"Hurry. While it is stable," says Max.

A few of the non-mystics grab up the remaining supplies. Everyone rushes into the portal.

I run through right behind Tammy. She stretches forward away from me as the jungle greenery seems to glide closer. The foliage snaps back, leaving me with a sensation like I'm running on greased ice, unable to move forward or back. A sudden, severe yank drags me sideways—everything going black.

The next thing I know, I spill forward onto my hands and knees upon warm, coarse dirt... more like tiny stones, or gravel, or like the grit from the bottom of a fish tank. An overwhelming stench like burning sulfur hangs in the air. I look down at black crumbles between my hands. Yeah, totally like the stuff from a fish tank.

"What the heck?"

I sit back and look around at a black-walled cave dotted with horned stalagmites. Grunts, gurgles, pig noises, and anguished screams echo from both directions. Oh, what the heck? Did I land in a telemarketing company office?

No, wait. This place isn't giving off anywhere near that level of evil.

This is like an outer layer of literal Hell or something. Considering I don't see my kids or the others, I should be thankful this weird sideways yank only affected me. My warning sense goes off, but not in a 'you're about to die horribly' way. I draw my sword and stomp forward, heeding the inexplicable notion it's the correct way for me to go.

A screeching potbellied creature leaps out from behind an onyx column in front of me. It's maybe five feet tall, naked, obviously male, with furry bird-like legs and stubby human arms. Long black claws curve from the digits of its three-fingered hands. Its head is more porcine than human, though last time I checked, hogs aren't supposed to have goat horns.

Whatever.

It's a demon. Don't really care how much sense it makes.

He runs in, trying to claw me. I slash his hand in defense, then follow up with a downward chop, striking him in the temple. The Devil Killer slices his flesh as if I hacked into a big, blobby Jell-O mold, stopping below the neck. Two halves of head droop away from each other to either side. The demon falls over backward and disintegrates into smoke.

"Amateurs." I tromp onward.

Another pig-man demon leaps out of a hole on the right, trying to tackle me. I stop short, let him face-plant the ground, then stab him in the side of the head. He explodes in a cloud of vapor. For the better part of the next ten minutes as I walk, these goobers keep flinging themselves at me. None of them are even close to dangerous, more annoying. Finally, the cave opens to a larger chamber, the left half of which is mostly a boiling tar lake. Not sure if it's actual tar, but it looks like it.

Seriously, what the eff is going on?

"You have made some enemies in low places, Sam," says the disembodied voice of Azrael. "They are going to continue harassing you whenever you cross the interstitial space."

"They're still butthurt about the Mindy Hogan deal?" I am, of course, referring to the zombie out-break in Arizona... instigated by the mother of all demons.

"Not so much for you helping the girl. An individual mortal means little to them. They seek revenge for the demon you destroyed."

I sigh. "So, you're basically saying every time I try to leap between dimensions, there's a chance I'm going to get kidnapped?"

"Essentially. While most demons are impulsive and quick to fury, seldom thinking of any conse-quences, they will continue harassing you until one of two things happen—either they defeat you, or you destroy so many of them, they begin to fear you."

I chuckle. "Didn't you basically 'apprentice' me as your demon killer?"

"I did."

"So, this is like termites summoning an exterminator right to their nest?"

"Your confidence is reassuring. Bascume the Unclean will not be expecting it."

A mild shudder runs down my spine. Nothing named 'the unclean' will be pleasant. Then again, I've dealt with Anthony's underwear in the laundry. Does every ten-to-twelve-year-old boy go through a phase where they try to annihilate their briefs?

Another pig demon emerges from behind a stone pillar and comes running at me.

I stick my sword out, killing the damn thing so easily it's almost like it obligingly impaled itself.

Wow, these demons have even less a sense of self-preservation than anyone who drives sleepy on the 405.

"Take the left passage," says Azrael.

I cross the open chamber and enter the cave to the left.

"Ma," says Anthony.

"Huh?" I spin. He's behind me, once again in his Fire Warrior form. "What are you doing here?"

"I should be asking you the same thing," he says, walking over to me.

"Demons pulled me sideways when I entered the portal," I say. "Now how did you get here?"

He shrugs. "Wanted to find you. Felt like I could go to where you were if I wanted to, so I did. Mind over matter sort of thing. Tammy's kinda having a panic attack."

"Legit panic attack or just freaking out?"

"Just freaking out, but kinda bad freaking out." He looks around. "Maybe we should stop telling people to 'go to Hell.' This looks legit."

I chuckle. "C'mon. There's a demon I need to have a word with."

Anthony draws his new golden angel sword.

"Didn't I tell you not to accept swords from strange angels?"

He grins. "Technically, you didn't... but I know you're making a joke."

"Wow, you met Big Mike. Nice."

Anthony gives me side eye. "Not sure he'd like you calling him that. Makes him sound like a male stripper."

I bite my lip. "Oops. Yeah, you're right. I meant big like important. High up the food chain."

Another pig demon charges us from the right. Anthony slices it in half, its two flaming pieces hit the ground and tumble past me before they collapse into dark smoke.

"Yeah. I know what you meant but it made me think of *Magic Mike*," says Anthony.

My turn to give *him* side eye. "You watched that?"

"No. Just heard of it."

We follow the cave, every so often killing a pig demon.

"Ma, these things are like life-size gummi bears with a bad attitude."

I laugh. "Don't make fun of the demons or we'll end up having to deal with nastier ones."

The cave leads us to another open chamber, this one with a seven-story-tall ceiling. Hundreds of naked human bodies hang from chains upon dozens of onyx columns. All dead, most are missing limbs or heads. As there's no point to torture a corpse, I'm assuming they're either decoration or snacks for the enormous creature presently sliding around the chamber.

I'm assuming it's Bascume the Unclean. From the waist up, he resembles a morbidly obese fifty-something man the size of a small office building, with thick, rear-curved ram horns. His pallid skin is coated in a layer of clear slime oozing over his multiple fat rolls before glooping to the ground, likely providing the lubrication for him to slide around on his massive fleshy tail. As far as I can tell, he has no legs or any other defined limbs below the waist, being essentially a centaur version of a giant slug.

He plucks a partial torso from a column and devours it. So much for the decoration theory.

"Okay, that's disgusting," says Anthony.

"Azrael, are you still listening?" I ask. "I'm going to need about twelve tons of salt."

My son summons his golden wings. "Ready?"

I unfurl my own black wings. "Yep."

We leap into the air since his head's about four stories high.

Seeing the massive demon is bad enough, but the true horror doesn't hit me until we get close enough to smell him. An aura of foulness surrounds

Bascume that I can only describe as a mixture of boiling rotten cheese, unflushed toilet, vomit, and the smell of a well-used garbage dumpster sitting outside in August.

The *only* good thing about this fight is Bascume appears incapable of moving faster than a human's walking pace… and he's only even going that fast due to being the size of a small office building. Were he not gigantic, he'd probably take two hours to cross the average living room.

Upon noticing us, Bascume emits a deep, baritone laugh while slapping himself on the belly. Slender, grey-skinned demons squeeze out from under his fat rolls like maggots tumbling from a disturbed corpse. They sprout wings of their own and leap into the air.

These are much faster than the pig ones, and they're so skinny it's like slashing a sword into a leather sack of broom handles. They're pretty fast though, and nip me with their claws a couple times. Fortunately, they're brittle and only one of them survived more than a single hit—because I lopped one of its wings off. He died on impact with the floor.

Bascume struggles to keep facing us as we circle him, his primary mode of attack being a firehose of dark green, flaming vomit. I don't care how dangerous or trivial it is, I'm *not* getting hit by something so incredibly disgusting. Not only is sticky, green, *flaming,* vomit bad enough… but it's loaded with giant bugs, which I'm sure will bite.

Once we clear the air of demons, Anthony and I begin to make strafing passes at Bascume's head... all while dodging the vomit. I feel like one of the little biplanes in *King Kong*, dodging these enormous, flabby arms. Spittle and green vomit roll down the demon's beard. Of course, it's not *actual* beard hair, but long, black serpents—also trying to bite us.

Good grief, Tammy is either going to instantly throw up when she sees this memory or crawl under her bed and stay there forever.

Anthony slices off one of Bascume's fingers. Honestly, the dull thump of a telephone-pole sized flesh log hitting the ground is way more disgusting than I'd imagined it could be. The demon slaps his gut again, squeezing out another batch of skinny demons from concealed pores.

"More zit demons incoming!" yells Anthony.

Of course, he's referring to how the big demon is squeezing them out of his pores. Nope. Not even holding that thought or I'm going to be throwing up, too.

We distance from the big guy to deal with the flying ones. Having Anthony here is a huge help. I probably could've handled these guys alone, but I'd have been a mess of small scratches. We beat the snot out of the flyers, killing all of them in under a minute, then dive again at the big guy. Anthony gets the idea to aim for his back. The centaur-slug shape of his body leaves him wide open there... like how a big bodybuilder can't reach behind himself to get rid of a kick-me sign.

Problem being, the dude is the size of a building. I really don't want to go down his throat to reach the heart. Patches of fire ignite on his huge, slimy body wherever Anthony cuts him open. Yellow pus rather than blood rolls out. The rotten Swiss cheese smell intensifies. I swoop around in front and stab at his chest on a literal flyby.

Anthony gives up on the defenseless back, the fat, bone, and gristle in the way is too thick to let us inflict more than superficial slices. Seemingly at random, my son stabs at one of the entity's gaping pores as he flies by it, his fiery sword plunging in to the cross-guard. Like holding a lit match to the opening of a gasoline can, a blast of fire shoots out of the orifice, then sucks backward into the demon's belly.

My inner alarm rages.

"Move!" I shout to my son.

The Fire Warrior spins and zooms to the side.

Bascume flails his arms, roaring in anguish—then explodes with a booming splatter.

Or at least, some of him explodes. A large portion of his belly and chest blasts outward in a rain of smoldering red gore and strands of gelatinous yellow fat. Dozens of half-formed skinny flying demons dangle from glands... or something. Bascume slumps—somewhat—to the left, the size and shape of his body preventing him from truly falling over.

My gaze falls on a pale grey lump pulsing in the

manner of a heart, deep inside his belly—not where a heart should be. Prior to the vapor explosion blowing his front half off, a twelve-foot-thick layer of blubber and demon-secreting pores stood between his skin and heart. Yeah, the Devil Killer is way impressive and all, but it's only so long.

Not like my son's new angel sword, which dwarfs it.

I dart in and stab the twitching, partially burned, heart. The organ—which is bigger than a phone booth—blackens entirely in three seconds. Expecting a massive blast of slime, I teleport straight up near the ceiling. Thus far, whenever I've killed a demon, there's been a crap-ton of hot, sticky slime showering everywhere. The last time I ended up covered in demonic blood. Getting rid of it felt like a full-body waxing.

Bascume doesn't burst, disintegrate, or even fall over. His mammoth body merely turns somewhat greyer, his insides darkening. Got a feeling this corpse is going to sit here for a long, long time. Maybe it'll petrify to stone. Awesome. No slime. Hmm. Guess it's different killing them in Hell.

A white portal opens at the far end of the room. Convenient.

No, I don't think killing the big demon made it open like something out of a video game. I merely did what Azrael wanted me to do and he's sending me an interdimensional Uber. Not wanting to suffer the reek of this place any longer, I dive toward the portal, grabbing Anthony's hand along the way.

Weird, it doesn't burn me.

"Nice sword," I say. "I've always called you an angel, but it seems it's getting a bit more literal these days."

"Seems that way." He glances at the flaming blade. I wonder where his other two blades went, those that seemed like extensions of his hands. Probably they got replaced by this much nicer sword. And by nicer, I mean badass.

I look up at my son's face. Or at least, at the face of the fiery being my son is currently embodying. An unexpected poke of guilt makes me look down. "What did I do to you, Ant?"

"You saved my life. Any mother would have." He shrinks into his normal form, then hugs me. "Remember that, Ma. You saved my life. I think maybe the reason I got sick is so you could do exactly what you did. Otherwise, *this* might not have happened."

"Destiny, huh? Why did they want my little boy out of all the little boys on Earth?"

"Who knows? And no, I'm not gonna go anywhere. At least, not yet. Gotta keep an eye on Tam. Besides, can't get a job with the seraphim without a high school diploma."

I chuckle. It sounds so silly, yet... wow. Another day, more weird.

"Let's go home?"

"Yeah."

We step into the portal at the same time.

I appear in a pure white place, featureless in

every direction.

Azrael is waiting for me a short distance ahead, smiling. Anthony's not here. Hopefully, he went back to the normal world. I'm alone with the Angel of Death.

Oh, boy.

Chapter Nineteen
Performance Meeting

"Your children and associates are fine," says Azrael.

I look around again at all the white space. "So, what is this? Like an annual performance review with my boss?"

Azrael chuckles. "Not exactly. You have questions."

"Doesn't everyone?"

"Yes, but few ever find answers or even truly know what their questions are."

"Whoa." I blink. "Wasn't ready for this level of deep."

He smiles. "To answer your questions, dark masters still exist. Those who were loyal to Elizabeth may withdraw to her fifth-dimension sanctum and ascend. It is more likely they fear their own mortality too much even to claim their full power. Most will return to the Earth and resume their existence as vampires, werewolves, and other creatures, forever trying to evade the cycle."

I nod.

"Supernatural creatures will still exist. Dark masters roamed the Earth before Elizabeth, and they will do so after her. She led a fraction of them. Elizabeth did not create them. She exploited their existence to defy the cycle of creation and seek power for herself. Demons still exist. Your work here is not done."

"What am I supposed to do now?" I pause, stuck on the realization Elizabeth must truly be gone if Azrael says so. A force who had so much influence over my reality for so long... gone. It's going to take a while to sink in. It's weird of me to feel this way, but some part of me—despite living in constant fear for the last two years of what she'd do to my kids—misses her. "Wasn't she my whole reason for existing as this... whatever I am?"

"No." Azrael chuckles. "It was never your fate to contain her. You already realized she manipulated you. Humans continually ask why do they exist because they didn't like the answer we gave them years ago."

I raise both eyebrows. "Wait, you mean there *is* an answer to that question?"

"Of course." He glances off to the side, faintly smiling.

"Mind telling me?"

"Humans exist because you exist."

I blink. Not sure if he's being serious or messing with me. "Umm…"

"The purpose of humans is to enjoy life and try to be nice to each other."

"Really?" I go to scratch my head and realize I'm still holding the Devil Killer, so I put it away, *then* scratch my head. "That's it? There's no greater purpose to it?"

"Why does there need to be? Life is beauty. No one asks why the sun burns or why rocks and mud are not the same thing. Humanity wastes far too much time worrying about pointless things."

I exhale and look down. "So, we exist. I should just enjoy whatever time I have left before I return to the Origin."

Azrael nods. "Enjoying one's existence *is* a purpose. You were expecting something more grand? More meaningful?" He gestures to the side. An image forms of four-year-old Tammy curled up beside me after I'd been shot. At the time, I'd been in a ton of pain, and didn't really notice the 'OMG you almost died' look in her eyes. Also, it never occurred to me a child her age could even contemplate death. "Look into her eyes. Do you see anything more meaningful to her than your mere existence?"

I wipe a tear. "No… Azrael, *am* I going to return to the Origin? I don't have a dark master anymore."

"Do you want to keep going around and around?" Azrael tilts his head at me.

"Oblivion is kinda scary... But, even if I reincarnated, I wouldn't remember my past existence, so I guess it really doesn't matter. In the end, it'll feel the same to me."

He clasps his hands in front of himself. "There you go. No reason to worry about things you cannot control, especially when they do not matter. Worry about meaningful things."

"Yeah... how am I going to handle Tammy being elderly? I assume Anthony is immortal."

"You assume correctly. Regarding Tammy, I'm sure you will find a way. You always do, Samantha. Remember, she's still a young woman with her entire life ahead of her."

"True."

"Take a few weeks off. Enjoy life. See where Earth takes you." He turns as if to leave, but pauses to say, "Oh, and check the toolshed."

I stare at the departing angel for a few seconds, bewildered. "Say again?"

Azrael keeps walking away, not turning to look back at me. "Someone will soon hire you to find a missing dog. Check the toolshed."

He fades invisible and disappears.

I stand there in silence, surrounded by immaculate whiteness in every direction, and a door-sized portal a short distance away on my left.

So, Elizabeth really is gone. The great moment —facing her—that had defined my life for so many years has finally come and gone.

Huh. How about that? I'd expected a bit more

fanfare. For what it's worth, I hope she found peace, at least for a little while before she ceased to be. Oh, well. Don't wanna keep Fido waiting. I gaze around at the nothingness one last time, and walk into the glowing doorway.

My son's immortal...

Yeah, kinda figured that.

Chapter Twenty
Exit Point

Anthony appears in the Venezuelan jungle—right in the middle of everyone.

Light Warriors, Max, Tam, and Allison all look at him. Despite the awkwardness of the Fire Warrior yet again shredding his clothes, he keeps his chin up and tries not to act as embarrassed as he feels, grabbing the closest palm frond to cover himself. Worst was having Allison see him in such a compromising position. Not that he'd ever act on it, but he crushed on her *so* bad. Sort of the way his friend Topher crushed on Ariana Grande. Zero expectation of anything ever happening, but... yeah.

Allison gestured at him, summoning an illusion of clothing.

He relaxes, tossing the big leaf away, wondering if his angelic powers include summoning stuff to wear?

With the awkwardness gone, he realizes his

mother wasn't standing next to him. Before worry sets in, he somehow knows she'd been pulled aside by Azrael for a quick chat. Tammy dashes over, almost hugging him, but she stops herself upon remembering he's wearing only illusions.

"Where's Mom?" she asks, her voice painfully desperate.

"She's fine. Talking to Azrael. Shouldn't be long."

"Oh." Tammy slouches. "What happened to you guys?"

"Demons sidetracked her. Me, too. We had to —"

"Gross!" She gags. "Why did you make me see that?"

"I, uhh, didn't. You looked."

Tammy clamps a hand over her mouth, trying not to throw up. Typical Tam. She did something then blamed him for it without *truly* blaming him for it. More generally complaining at having seen or experienced something. Not his problem.

Max approaches. "Where is your mother?"

"Talking to Azrael."

"Ahh, yes." He gazes up, then nods. "Anthony, I was wondering if you might consider joining my school?"

"Are you seriously 'Professor-X'-ing my brother?" asks Tammy. But she knows the question was coming. They all did. Heck, Anthony is surprised it took this long. Then again, he suspects Max had waited for the right time. And the death of his mother was that time.

Max chuckles. "In a way, yes. I always expected the confrontation with my mother would be my exit point." He looks at Anthony. "But you kept me around, kid. The least you can do is go to my school."

"Exit point?" asked Tammy. "Oh, you... wait, you *wanted* to die?"

"Want and acceptance are not the same thing." Max smiles. "I merely figured the machinery of the universe allowed me to extend my life as a sort of counterbalance to Elizabeth. It seemed proper that the two of us met our ends at the same time."

Anthony takes in some air. "Well, I've been thinking about it."

"Ordinary school isn't going to do you any good, son. Your life is on a course far more important than whiling away the days in a cubicle under fluorescent lights."

"Is it really in the center of the Earth?"

"Close to it."

"Can I, like, come home on the weekends or something?"

Max claps him on the shoulder. "As often as you want. Well, within reason. There is, after all, much to learn. Think of it as a sort of prerequisite to becoming an angel."

"Sounds good to me. The hard part will be convincing Mom." Anthony grins.

"Oh, I think I know how to talk to her." Max winked.

Chapter Twenty-one
Little Bit Clingy

Talk about a weird feeling.

It's been two days since I reappeared in the Venezuelan jungle and teleported everyone back to California. Despite our victory over Elizabeth, the Light Warriors were somber. Of the seventy-two who'd gone with us, eighteen died. Given the power of the ascendant dark masters, it's honestly an impressively good result for mostly ordinary mortals.

Tammy has been under my skirt like a six-year-old ever since we returned home. Not like crying or clinging or scared, more like just wanting to be around me. Being in our house reminded her of the scenario watching her alternate self melt down, and worsened her guilt at being bratty a few years ago. At least she hasn't taken it to the point of wanting to sleep in my bed at night.

She beans me with a small couch pillow. "I'm not *that* bad. Just... grateful. You know how they say 'you don't know what you got until it's gone?' Yeah. Watching that other version of me made me realize what I had."

I reach out and hug her... because, yeah, she's sitting that close to me.

Tammy laughs. "I'm gonna try to get into a college close enough to stay living here. Maybe Cal State Fullerton. Most of my friends are staying local. Only Paige is talking about going to school out of state, but she still might not. It sucks being far away from all your friends and family."

"Some people *like* taking adventures."

"Yeah, but I'm not one of those people. Does it bother you if I get a little clingy for a while? The 'out-of-control druggie nightmare me' is really messing with my head. I keep hearing the *thud*."

I shudder. Her reminding me of a version of my daughter head-butting a truck at ninety miles an hour makes me grab her. "I should have asked Azrael to wipe that memory out of my head. Maybe yours, too."

"It's okay, Ma. I think I needed to see that. Helps me sorta get my head on straighter. Makes me want to do more with my life."

"That makes me happy," I say. "More than you know."

"Oh, I know."

"This feels so weird," says Anthony from the nearby recliner, where he'd been sitting quietly with his eyes half-closed.

"Being an angel-in-training?" I ask.

"That, too. But I mean *not* worrying what Elizabeth is cooking up." He rolls his head to look at me. "It's like we're finally free. Don't have to worry about some horrible thing happening to us out of nowhere at any moment."

I sink into the sofa with Tammy still in my arms. "Yeah. It is nice not having to be hyper-vigilant all the time. Going to take me months to relax."

"Demons are still after you," says Tammy.

"Gee, thanks for reminding me."

Anthony suddenly stands. "It's more difficult than you think for them to enter our world. Maybe I should bless the house so they can't get in."

Tammy raises an eyebrow. "Seriously, you can do that?" Her expression of curious interest shifts to panic. "Oh, God. No. Don't you dare f—"

My son expels gas so loud a car alarm outside goes off... well, almost. The car alarm just happened to go off. Merely a case of perfect coincidental timing. However, Anthony is guaranteed to send Topher a text claiming to have triggered the alarm.

Tammy holds her breath and runs to open the front door. I stand, spread my wings, and flap to clear the air.

"Aww, Mom, it's not *that* bad," says Anthony.

Chapter Twenty-two
Mom Mode

So, it's Wednesday, three days after our return from Venezuela.

Anthony wants to transfer to Max's school. I'm torn. On one hand, I want him to have as normal a life as possible, which includes the high school experience. Then again, Max's school *is* a legit school even if it's kinda closer to Hogwarts than anything. He'll still have the experience there, and even be among teens more like him… or at least ones he can talk to about 'the weird stuff' openly.

Max confirms that they do real school work there, too, among all the other craziness. His school is linked to real schools around the globe, all of which provide real documentation and diplomas. Only, the "physical" schools have portals to the real school somewhere in the center of the earth.

Okay, maybe it is better for him to go there. Do

we transfer him in the middle of the school year or wait until his junior year? Max said the transfer *appears* legitimate, which has me worrying his school isn't actually legitimate. Then again, what government official would accredit 'magical studies' without whiskey or weed being involved?

I was assured that all paperwork is legit, and passes muster to any and all state and federal departments, in this country and others. I guess the most important thing here is that my son would learn of the evils in this world, and how to fight them. Of course, being an angel-in-training, he had a leg up—or a wing up—on his fellow classmates. Knowing my son, he wouldn't let that go to his head.

It's 3:26 in the afternoon and he's presently at Jacky's Gym. Emmett Floyd, Kingsley's werewolf friend, has taken over as the manager for the time being. Ant might be content to let the guy run the place for the foreseeable future rather than step in as manager. I suspect his life is going to make random demands of his time, so it's good to have someone there to keep the place running. My son views the gym as a living memorial to Jacky, hence not changing the name or changing much of anything about it.

Tammy's still obsessing over her other self, though less and less. At present, she's in her room hanging out with Dana, Ankita, Renee, Ari, and Veronica. Tomorrow, she's going to try returning to her job at Wendy's.

My cell phone rings. Would this finally be the lady calling about the missing dog?

"This is Sam," I say, by way of answering.

"Miss Moon?" asks a whispery child's voice.

"You got her."

"Dunno if you remember me. It's Paxton."

"Of course I remember you. What's wrong? You sound upset."

She pauses, sniffling.

After ten seconds, I ask, "Paxton?"

"Sorry," she whispers super quiet. "Someone was close."

I sit up. "Are you in danger?"

"Kinda, yeah." She bites back a sob. "My dad lied to the cops. He somehow convinced them I tripped and fell down the stairs trying to run away from home. They're going to send me back to him. I don't wanna go. He's gonna kill me. You said I could call you if I needed help."

"Totally." I narrow my eyes. "Where are you now?"

"Hiding under the bed in another room at the shelter so no one can find me."

"I'm on my way."

She whispers, "Thank you!"

"Don't hang up, okay?"

"Okay."

I close my eyes and picture the room where I met her. The dancing flame appears in a field of blackness. It rushes toward me, even as I move toward it...

I'm in a darkened room full of bunk beds. Luck is with me; no one else is here, including Paxton. At this hour, the displaced teens who live here are probably out at their part-time jobs, maybe in counseling sessions, or elsewhere in the shelter. The TV-and-game room is a lot more entertaining than a space full of sagging beds.

"Pax?" I say into the phone.

"Yeah?" she whispers.

"Can you go back to the room where we first met?"

"Why?"

"I'll explain later. Trust me."

She doesn't say anything back, but I can almost sense her nodding.

Twenty seconds later, the door opens and she pokes her head inside. I wave.

"Sam?"

"The one and only."

Her eyes are the same reddish-pink as the dress she's wearing, her face wet with tears. She practically faints at the sight of me, grabbing her mouth in both hands. A bracelet on her right wrist, a bunch of plastic 'crystal' hearts, slips halfway down her arm.

Paxton looks at me the way a kid might look at a firefighter kicking in the door of their burning house. Once she processes me being here, she runs over and grabs me, trembling. Her thoughts are a scramble of panic. The only reason she thinks her father would demand she come home is so he can punish her. The things he called her while throwing her around her bedroom after catching her kissing another girl... yeah, I don't understand why he'd want her back, either. Unless he lied about her injuries to avoid prosecution for child abuse. What kind of heartless bastard of an investigator believed *his* version of the story?

"Please don't let him kill me," whispers Paxton.

I sit on the edge of the nearest bed, comforting her, reassuring her repeatedly I won't allow anyone to hurt her. It takes about twenty minutes, but she eventually stops trembling. If this girl had claws, she'd be digging them in to hold onto me for dear life. She's not acting at all. Her thoughts are full of dread. In her mind, her father's screaming at her over and over again.

"Pax?" I ask. "Question for you."

She leans back, peering up at me. "Yeah?"

"How would you feel about... me becoming your foster mom?"

"Really?" Paxton stares at me. "You'd do that?"

"Absolutely."

"Why are you angry?"

Whoa. The kid might be an empath. "Thinking about your father and what he did to you."

My mama bear mode is going into overdrive looking into this kid's innocent face and wounded blue eyes. "Do you really think your father intends to hurt you?"

She fidgets. "I dunno. When he was screaming, he said people like me deserve to die, but I dunno if he's gonna do it on purpose. Just, you know, get so mad and hit me harder than he means to. He's huge. And I'm, well, not. Do the math. I don't wanna live in fear like that all the time. If they send me back there, I'm just gonna run away."

This girl is a twig, no doubt. Even a normal adult man hitting her could do serious damage. I'm sure there's a little fear distortion going on in her mind right now, but her father looks like a weight-lifter. He works construction, apparently. Her memories have way too many moments of abuse, though mostly emotional, yelling and so on, but a few cases of violence. Yeah, if he ever hit Paxton out of rage, he'd kill her. I can't sit back and allow her to go back to an environment like that. Everything in her head convinces me he's going to kill her, intentionally or not.

"No, you won't. You said you'd like to have a mother like me. If you're serious, I can make it happen."

"How?"

"Well, I have a few tricks up my sleeve. But fair warning, if you stay with me, things might get a little… unusual."

She tilts her head. "What do you mean?"

"Nothing major… magic, demons, immortals, unpredictable supernatural stuff. It might be danger-ous, but I've managed to keep my two other kids alive this long."

Paxton laughs. "You're teasing me."

"Nope."

"Wait, you're being serious?"

"Totally and completely." I extend my wings.

"Whoa... they're so pretty!" She reaches out and touches one. "I could kinda tell you weren't lying, but wow..."

I watch her 'pet' my wing for a moment, then say, "My life is full of stuff like this. I'm currently at war with demons. Vampires are real. So are werewolves. I'll do my best to shield you from the strangest stuff, but there's a chance you'll see things most people don't believe in."

"It's okay. I can tell you want to protect me. My dad never felt like you do when I got scared. He just wanted me to stop crying as fast as possible."

"Dang." I sigh. "What happened to your mom?"

"He said she died in a car accident when I was like two."

"I'm sorry, sweetie. Okay, consider yourself the kitten I couldn't resist taking home."

She manages a feeble smile and makes a soft, "Mew."

"Last chance. It's not fair to spring all this paranormal stuff on you if you aren't able and willing to deal with it. If you'd rather not, I'll erase the memory of you seeing my wings, take care of your dad, and get you placed somewhere safe. If you want to be part of my crazy world..." I offer her my hand.

Paxton grabs it without hesitation, her stare pleading. "I can totally feel how much you wanna protect me. And I don't have to hide who I am with you, either."

"You're an empath."

"I think so." She shrugs one shoulder.

A black woman in her late twenties barges in. "There you are! Pax baby, you know you gotta go home. Girl, what you doing?"

Before I can say anything, Paxton hides behind me. "He's gonna hurt me. You know he will."

The woman sighs. "Cops will haul me out of here if I don't let them bring you back to your father. But you just call me if he lays one hand—"

"It's handled," I say, happy to see that Paxton has others in her corner.

"And who are you?"

I stare into the social worker's brain. "No one you remember seeing. The police already took Paxton."

The woman goes glassy-eyed. A moment later, she walks out.

"Holy crap," whispers Paxton. "Was that one of those 'tricks' you told me about?"

"Yep."

"Are you an angel?"

"Not sure. I used to be a vampire, but I got better."

She chuckles. "Are you teasing me or being serious?"

"Serious."

"I'm happy you got better."

"Thank you." I stand. "Now, go pack up your stuff. Time to go."

She gathers a few items of clothing from a small dresser, stuffing everything in a backpack as well as a plastic trash bag, likely the same one she used to bring her stuff here.

"What's your old address?" I ask.

"Why?" She freezes. "Are you gonna hurt him?"

I rub my chin. "Tempted to throw him down the stairs, but nah. It wouldn't solve anything and wouldn't really make me feel better. No, I'm going to compel him to sign away his parental rights. Plus, we need to get the rest of your stuff from your old room."

Paxton stands, slinging her backpack over one shoulder. "What about judges and social workers?"

"My boyfriend is a lawyer. He'll handle everything. Oh, and he's a werewolf."

She opens her mouth to say something, but emits an "Eep!" before gazing around at the ceiling.

"Oh, he's not so bad. Think of a big fluffy dog."

"No, not that. I eeped because I'm hearing voices now."

OMG, Mom, says Tammy. *She's like totes adorbs.*

I chuckle. "That voice in your head? Say hi to your new sister, Tammy. She's telepathic."

"Wow, you weren't kidding about the super-natural stuff, were you?"

"I was not."

Paxton gives me her old address.

I pull it up on Google Maps via my phone, pop

down to street view, and get a look at the front of the house.

When I hold my hand out again, Paxton grasps it.

I summon the dancing flame.

Chapter Twenty-three
Peace

We appear on the front lawn.

The small, two-story house has a full porch with four steps. The bottom three still have blood on them. Paxton nearly faints at the sudden change of scenery.

I hold her up. "Sorry, I should have warned you."

"So weird," whispers Paxton. "Did we really just do that?"

"We did. How do you think I got to the shelter so fast?"

"Oh, right." She turns her head to look at me. "He isn't gonna be here now. Still at work."

"Okay. Good chance to get your stuff then. I can come back and deal with him later."

She still has keys to the place in her backpack. Paxton opens the front door and walks into the most bachelory bachelor pad I've ever seen. He's practically built a second La-Z-Boy out of empty Heineken beer cans. Paxton crosses the living room, but becomes strangely rigid halfway to the stairs.

"Pax? What's wrong?"

"Coffee table." She keeps walking past it, then gingerly goes up a set of hardwood stairs as if afraid to slip. It's the same stairs I saw her go down face-first in her memory.

I walk over to the actual recliner—not the beer can pile—and peer past it at the coffee table. Several pamphlets for conversion therapy sit on top of a pile of fantasy football magazines.

"Ignore it," I say.

She continues upstairs, and I follow.

Her bedroom is both adorable and a mess. Fluffy white bed, a handful of stuffed animals, lots of white and pink... but it also looks like a bar brawl happened in here. Two holes in the pink-painted drywall look about the size of a man's fist.

"We can keep whatever you want," I say.

"Cool. Even the bed?"

"If you want. Though it's not going to be easy to teleport with that sucker. Grab the basics for now. We can come back with a moving van later."

"Okay." She darts around, gathering stuff of high importance. Clothes, simple jewelry, favorite dolls and fluffy slippers... you know, vitals.

Wham. The entire house shakes.

Paxton yelps, then stares at me with pure dread, whispering, "He's home. Must've got off work early."

"Don't worry. It doesn't matter how big he is."

"Someone up there?" bellows a man. "Pax? Those idiots drop you off alone?"

"Not exactly," I holler back, and step into the hallway.

A muscular bald guy, a touch shy of six feet tall, stomps up the stairs. He sees me and pauses, confused. "You a social worker?"

"In a way. I'm here to take custody of Paxton from you."

"The hell you are." He storms over and grabs my shirt.

"Mr. Deering, that's assault."

"You're in my damn house. You're lucky I don't—"

I punch him in the chest, hard enough to knock the wind out of him and send him flying over backward but not break anything. At least, I don't think.

Paxton gasps.

He rolls onto his side, gawping for air.

Okay, I lied. Hitting him made me feel a lot better. I stoop over him, grab his shirt collar, and pull him up to make eye contact. He goes limp the instant my mental powers hammer his brain. Yeah, he totally lied to get out of jail, claiming Paxton had a tantrum and tripped down the stairs trying to run away from home. Digging deeper, I discover he accidentally killed his wife eleven years ago by hitting her too hard in the kitchen during an argument. Some of his buddies helped him stage a car accident.

Oh, you son of a bitch.

Fortunately, he's not planning to kill Paxton on purpose, but I can see the guy easily losing control if she refuses to 'straighten' up. And, yeah, living with this guy is going to completely mess her up for life.

I crack my knuckles, implanting a command for him to go to the nearest police station and confess to killing his wife. Then, he's going to admit he hurled Paxton down the stairs, dragged her across the living room, and literally threw her out of the house. The only reason Paxton's girlfriend escaped injury is she climbed out the bedroom window.

Instead of venting my anger at this guy with physical violence, I pour it into the strength of the mental commands.

Wait a second. Sherbet's homicide.

I alter my command so this guy goes to Sherbet's precinct. Pretty sure he'd be willing to take lead on the investigation into the death of Paxton's mother. Also kinda have a feeling he won't be too fond of a suspect who brutalized his daughter for being gay.

Once I'm done with mind surgery, I go back into the pink bedroom.

Paxton's curled up on the floor between the bed and the wall, hiding and crying.

"It's okay. He won't be a problem."

She looks up at me in total shock. "But how…?"

"Supernatural stuff, kiddo." I grin. "Got everything you need for a couple days?"

Paxton exhales, wipes her face, and stands. She's totally bewildered that her father didn't beat the crap out of me, and thinking she might just like all this 'supernatural stuff' after all.

I hold out a hand. "C'mon, Pax. Let's go home."

She gathers up her things, hurries over, and takes my hand.

Eyes closed, I picture my living room—and summon the dancing flame.

The Moon family just became a little bigger.

And I couldn't be happier.

The End

J.R. RAIN AND MATTHEW S. COX

To be continued in:

Vampire Train
Vampire for Hire #22
Coming soon!

About J.R. Rain:

J.R. Rain is an ex-private investigator who now writes full-time. He lives in a small house on a small island with his small dog, Sadie. Please visit him at www.jrrain.com.

About Matthew S. Cox:

Originally from South Amboy NJ, **Matthew S. Cox** has been creating science fiction and fantasy worlds for most of his reasoning life. Since 1996, he has developed the "Divergent Fates" world, in which Division Zero, Virtual Immortality, The Awakened Series, The Harmony Paradox, and the Daughter of Mars series take place.

Matthew is an avid gamer, a recovered WoW addict, Gamemaster for two custom systems, and a fan of anime, British humour, and intellectual science fiction that questions the nature of reality, life, and what happens after it.

He is also fond of cats.

Please find him at: www.matthewcoxbooks.com

Made in the USA
Monee, IL
06 September 2020